MURDER MYSTERY AT THE INN

Inn Vermont Cozy Mysteries, Book 3

THEA CAMBERT

Summer Prescott Books Publishing

Copyright 2021 Summer Prescott Books

All Rights Reserved. No part of this publication nor any of the information herein may be quoted from, nor reproduced, in any form, including but not limited to: printing, scanning, photocopying, or any other printed, digital, or audio formats, without prior express written consent of the copyright holder.

**This book is a work of fiction. Any similarities to persons, living or dead, places of business, or situations past or present, is completely unintentional.

Chapter One

Being an innkeeper sounds like one of those fantasy jobs, right? You spend your days greeting guests, baking muffins, and decorating the place for whatever holiday is coming. Well, in reality, you *do* greet guests, bake muffins, and decorate—in between all the cleaning, maintaining, marketing, and wracking your brain to come up with new and interesting ideas that will get the customers excited about visiting your inn.

Normally, at the Inn at Pumpkin Hill in the tiny town of Williamsbridge, Vermont, we don't have to lift a finger to attract guests from around mid-September to the end of October. That's because the village is nestled right into the heart of the Green Mountains—a short distance north of Montpelier, but south of Stowe—and the glorious fall foliage is all the publicity we need. The leaf peepers descend on the village, swelling the population, filling up the shops, the restaurants, and yes, the inns, to capacity. While Williamsbridge doesn't rely fully on tourism to keep its economy afloat, there are many of us who count on the influx of visitors during certain seasons—most especially the fall.

I grew up on Pumpkin Hill—appropriately named because at this time of year, we have pumpkins scattered all over the place. I mean, you can't take a walk without tripping over one. It's been that way since forever. As a child, I lived with my parents in the main house, scampering up and down the hill and running through the woods that surround us with my best friend, Matthew Stewart. The house—which my parents smartly converted to an inn as a way of maintaining the place and keeping it in the family after many generations—was built shortly after the town itself was founded in 1763. Behind the house at the edge of the woods lies the little caretaker's cottage, and that's where I live now. I moved away from the village for only a short time to go to college and earn my master's degree in journalism. Then I moved home—not because I couldn't have lived elsewhere, but because I love this town. I love the kitschy shops, the quaint restaurants, the maple trees that grow up and down the streets . . . I love Picadilee Park at the town square, and Cottontail Creek that runs parallel to High Street . . . I even love the fact that our town was named Williamsbridge because the founder, William Hadley, built a bridge over the creek, and everyone around found their way here and there based on that simple landmark. (You're looking for the Jones Farm? It's just south of William's bridge. The flour mill? Over William's bridge and down the creek.) Most of all, I love the people who live here. I count them all family—from my crotchety editor at the newspaper, Walter Wright, to my friend Edna Hillsborough, who owns Potbelly's Soup Kitchen, to my godmother and the queen of all things maple sugar, Evvy Sumner.

A few years ago, my father passed away, leaving Mom to run the inn alone. Around last Christmas, Mom asked me if I'd like to become her official partner. I had already been helping out as much as I could, but Mom was proposing that I really make the inn my job, in addition to my work at the newspaper. She would teach me the ins and outs of the business, and who knows? One day, I might run the place myself and raise another generation of Lewis children there.

After college but before I came to work at the inn, I had been living in a tiny apartment above my friend Edna's garage, scraping by on my small-town rookie journalist's salary. I was determined not to just move into my old room back home. But when Mom made the proposal that I work at the inn, it included lodging in the caretaker's cottage. My rent is covered as part of my salary, and I maintain a measure of independence to boot.

My aforementioned best friend, Matthew Stewart, rounds out our staff. After Dad died, Matthew started picking up the slack at the inn. We never asked him to, but Matthew's just that kind of guy. He's an aspiring novelist. He holds a master's in creative writing. But like me, steady work as a writer is still just out of reach. Mom decided to make Matthew part of the staff as well, and to be honest, neither of us could imagine what we'd do without him. He helps with literally everything, from mowing to mending to repairing, and even helps me brainstorm about marketing.

That's how he and I came up with the idea for our Pumpkin Hill Murder Mystery Weekend. For whatever reason—most likely in part due to climate change and rainfall totals that year—the leaves weren't quite as vibrant as usual, so we weren't drawing our typical abundance of leaf peepers. The town still needed that annual autumn boost in revenue, so we put our heads together and did some research, and found that murder mystery getaways were seriously trending. We would dress the inn up, giving it a Halloween-Agatha Christie vibe, and concoct a mystery that included the whole village. Everyone from shop owners to restaurants would have a part to play, and all of us would benefit from the increase in business.

"Are you two sure this is a good idea?" Mom asked, coming into the family room as Matthew and I propped a giant bulletin board onto an easel. "What's this?"

"Mom, do you know *nothing* about amateur sleuthing? This is our murder board," I said. "This is where our detectives will be able to pin up clues and suspect names during the weekend, to help them solve *The Murder in the Haunted Village*."

"An Inn at Pumpkin Hill special event," Matthew added smartly.

Mom frowned. "Are we sure we want to even *hint* at the idea of murder? After all that's happened here?"

Okay. So recently, there have been a couple of bumps along the road for the Inn at Pumpkin Hill. Last Christmas, there was a family reunion where one guest was murdered . . . And then this past February, there was the little matter of yet another guest dying at the inn . . . who turned out to have been poisoned. But those crimes were solved—with Matthew's and my help—and there had been no more troubles all through the spring and summer.

"Mom, it's almost Halloween," I said.

"And murder mystery events are all the rage right now," said Matthew.

"The whole town's getting involved. And not only did we fill to capacity for this weekend, but so did several other places in town, all because of us." I gave Mom a nudge, and she softened a bit.

"So, the guests arrive Friday morning, and then the mystery gets underway Friday night?"

"Yep." I finished sticking pins into the bulletin board and then tacked on a sign at the top that read *Whodunnit? Pin Your Clues Here!*

"I'm probably just a little gun-shy," said Mom. Then she cleared her throat. "Bad choice of words."

"We're going outside to cut a few pumpkins for our jack-o'-lanterns that'll go on the front porch," I said. "I'll be back in to help with the baking in about half an hour."

"Good," said Mom. "Oh—and don't forget that Ian is coming for dinner tonight."

"Mom, this is the fifth time today you've reminded me."

Mom raised a brow at me and went off into the kitchen. She had been in good spirits even more so than usual since last winter, when Doc Jenkins—a.k.a. Ian—started coming around the inn more. Yep, my mother had a gentleman caller, who also happened to be one of her and my dad's oldest and dearest friends. They all grew up together. When Dad died a few years ago, Mom was only in her early fifties. Far too young to spend the rest of her life without a companion. I understood that in theory, of course. But in reality, seeing your mother beaming at the doctor who gave you all your checkups as a kid is a little bit weird. I kept having this feeling that he'd pull out a tongue depressor over a plate of toast one morning. Still, I was happy for Mom. And that particular dinner was a big deal because usually, Doc just came over for morning coffee or the occasional lunch. Dinner was different. It represented the next level. And since it meant a lot to Mom, it meant a lot to me, too.

"You're staying for dinner," I said to Matthew.

"Is that an invitation?" Matthew asked, taking off the red baseball cap he always wore, running his fingers through his dark, scruffy hair, and putting the cap back on.

"It's a command."

Matthew gave me a salute. "Okay. I'll stay," he said in a sort of gravelly voice.

Then he grinned and my heart felt like it skipped a beat, an irritating thing that's been happening for a while now. Matthew's my best friend. I'd never want anything to mess that up—not that I'm saying I've fallen for him. Not at all. It's just that I already love Matthew. So sometimes I get confused.

"Let's go get to those pumpkins," I said quickly, before he could possibly notice that my confounded cheeks were turning pink. "I want the front porch to look amazing."

Matthew was still grinning at me. "Don't worry. It will."

"Don't worry?" I echoed with a snort. "Do you have any idea who you're talking to?"

He pushed the door open and stood aside. "I'm talking to my Eloise, of course."

There might've been a time many years ago when I would've taken issue with him referring to me as *his* Eloise. But that day, it only warmed my heart. We went outside together into the bright autumn day, pulling an old red wagon along to fill with pumpkins.

Chapter Two

I really needed a free evening to catch up on my work for the newspaper. I'd gradually been taking on more responsibility there. I'd started out as a part-time features reporter. Then Walter began assigning more news articles and made me the newest Miss Smithers. Miss Smithers is Williamsbridge's beloved advice columnist—and not a soul, other than Walter and Miss Smithers herself, ever knows her identity. It's a long-running joke in Williamsbridge that when you spot a light up on one of the surrounding mountainsides at night, it's probably just Miss Smithers, watching over the town. She's that mysterious.

I'm actually the *fourth* Miss Smithers. Edna Hillsborough—the one who owns Potbelly's Soup Kitchen and whose garage apartment I used to live in—was the third. Part of the job is writing in the style of the original Miss Smithers. Edna deduced last winter that I had taken her place, so I guess there are three of us who know who Miss Smithers is in this case. Anyway, I couldn't resist taking the job when Walter offered it, and as a result, I feel like I have three jobs, between my regular assignments at the paper, running the inn with Mom, and the advice column.

Not to toot my own horn, but since I took the column, the letters have been pouring in. That's great, because Walter is happy and it also means my advice is well received and entertaining. But it's also bad, because I can never seem to get ahead of all the requests for help. It's really difficult to pick and choose who I'll answer and who I won't . . . and lately Walter's been thinking of making the column more than once a week. He's even talking about publishing the *Onlooker* four times a week instead of three, and letting Miss Smithers have a column in all four editions. The column sells papers, Walter says.

Which is amazing, but then again, it's a lot for me to keep all those plates spinning, never letting one fall to the ground. I don't want to let anyone down—not Walter, not Mom, not myself. So, every now and then, when things pile up, I get a little crazed. And unfortunately, I am the only person in town who can't ask Miss Smithers what to do about it.

"Eloise, what's wrong?" Mom asked that evening as we set the table together.

"Nothing." I might have snapped at her a little—in part because I hate it when people ask what's wrong when I'm feeling grumpy. And of course, I couldn't tell her what was wrong anyway.

Doc Jenkins had arrived and he and Matthew were outside looking at the gardens. We have a beautiful garden area to one side of the house, with little gravel paths running between the beds—that fall, filled with late-blooming fall flowers, herbs, and vegetables.

"You're acting like something's bothering you." Mom centered a cheery vase of black-eyed Susans on the table.

"Mom, I'm just—" I sighed. "I'm feeling a little overwhelmed at the moment."

"Because of me and Ian? Is it bothering you that I have a—" She stopped short of saying *boyfriend*, since Doc is a stone's throw from sixty, and that word didn't quite fit.

We'd said all this without realizing that Doc and Matthew had come in the back door, through the screened porch that adjoins the kitchen. Doc had clearly heard the exchange and looked concerned.

"Should I—" He came further into the room and stood by my mother, lowering his voice. "Is this not a good night to have our first official dinner together?"

"Absolutely not," said Mom. "I mean—it's *not* not a good night." She patted his hand and went into the kitchen.

I sighed and shook my head, then caught Matthew's eyes across the room. He gave me a look that clearly said, *Say something to smooth this over.*

"Oh, Doc, I was just telling Mom that I'm feeling overwhelmed with juggling my writing assignments for the paper with my work at the inn, especially with our murder mystery event coming up this weekend."

Doc nodded in understanding. Matthew looked satisfied. But from then on, the evening wasn't as relaxed as it should've been, and I thought it was probably because my tension was contagious. I couldn't help it. I needed to get back to my cottage and have a few hours to write and edit. And I always wear my emotions on the surface, though it would be really handy if I could learn to bury them a bit deeper. Doc ended up leaving at the soonest socially acceptable moment, right after a single slice of Mom's pumpkin pie with her salted brown butter pecans sprinkled on top and only one cup of coffee. Matthew followed close on his heels, and Mom was quieter than usual as we cleared away the dishes. I felt lousy, because I knew I'd messed up, but I still felt stressed about work. I hate it when my mother is disappointed in me, more than almost anything else.

"Sorry, Mom," I said as I collected the placemats from the table. "I shouldn't have brought my bad attitude to the evening."

"I don't understand why you're so much more stressed than usual," said Mom. "Has Walter assigned a lot more work this week or something? I mean, I read the *Onlooker*. From what I can tell, you're writing your usual number of articles."

Of course, I couldn't tell her than it was actually Miss Smithers that was the problem, so I just said, "No, I just let some things pile up and I need to get to work before I can go to bed tonight."

"Is working here at the inn too much for you, Eloise? Because if it is—"

"No! Of course not. I just have a lot to do. It's all good stuff. Just—it's a lot sometimes."

"It's important to me that you know that if it upsets you for me to be seeing Ian—"

"No!" I cut her off again. "Mom, I'm glad you have someone. And anyway, you shouldn't have to worry about what your twenty-seven-year-old daughter thinks about your love life."

"Almost twenty-eight," Mom said with a smile. "It'll be your birthday next Saturday."

That hit me like a ton of bricks. Twenty-eight is almost thirty. Thirty is practically thirty-five. And from there, forty is just around the corner. Forty isn't old these days. But Mom's little reminder made me suddenly think about the list of things I'd planned to accomplish by thirty. Successful journalist. Wife. Maybe even a mom . . . Thirty had seemed old when I was twenty. But now . . . "I'm going out to the cottage," I said, feeling a fresh wave of grumpiness—this one entirely self-induced.

Mom nodded. "See you tomorrow."

It would've been nice to stay and talk to her some more, to really and truly clear the air. It would've been nice to sit by the fire and drink cocoa and smooth things over. Or call Doc and Matthew back, and break out a board game. But I didn't do those things. Instead, I went out the back door, across the yard, and into my cottage, where I stewed and tried to figure out what was really bothering me, struggled to focus, wrote some half-hearted advice, and then climbed into bed, where I tossed and turned all night.

Chapter Three

I awoke early the next morning to someone banging on my front door. I'd been deeply asleep, lost in a dream where I was in the sea, treading water, and had come upon a boat. I was banging furiously on the side of it, hoping someone would pull me out of the water, but to no avail. I sat bolt upright in bed, realizing that the banging was real. I looked out of my second-floor bedroom window. The early blue-gray of twilight, before sunrise. I peered down at the ground near the front door. The knocker stepped back from the door and looked up. Matthew.

I wrapped myself in a fuzzy blanket, slipped my feet into my fleecy slippers, and tromped down the stairs. "Why could you possibly be here at this hour?"

Matthew came inside. "It's a big day. I wanted to make sure you were up."

"Since when do I need to be reminded to get up on time?"

"Still grumpy?"

"I *hate* it when people ask me if I'm grumpy when I'm—"

"Grumpy?"

"I, uh, didn't sleep well last night."

"Yep. I figured. That's why I was afraid you'd oversleep."

He steered me to my little kitchen table and sat me down, then flipped on my two-cup coffee maker. A few minutes later, he'd poured us each a cup and sat down next to me.

"You're really irritating you know," I said, but then took a sip and felt almost instantly better.

"Yeah, I get that a lot."

"From who?"

"Only you. Everyone else thinks I'm great."

"Yeah, well they don't know you as well as I do."

"That goes both ways, my friend," he said. "Now drink your coffee. We have to get ready for the onslaught. Today's the last day before our guests arrive, and I forgot to tell you we got another booking in last night."

"Another—so we're almost booked *solid*?"

He smiled and nodded over the rim of his mug. "The only room left is the little attic bedroom. Otherwise, we're full up."

"We have a lot to do today."

"Yep."

"I've got to go up and get dressed," I said, standing.

"For your coffee date," Matthew said.

"For my what?"

"You have a coffee date this morning at eight. At The Steamy Bean."

"The Steamy Bean? Have you lost your mind?" It was as though Matthew was speaking some other language. "I mean, I like The Steamy Bean, but why would I have a coffee date there? And with whom?"

"With Doc." Matthew picked up our cups, rinsed them, and set them in the sink.

"Hey—I wasn't done with—"

"You can get another cup at the coffee shop."

"Okay, but why am I . . ." I let my words fade as I thought for a moment—about Matthew, and how he hated conflict of any kind, and about last night, and how things hadn't gone as smoothly as they should have. "Did you actually call Doc and make this coffee date?"

"No. He's at The Steamy Bean every weekday morning a few minutes after eight. I thought you could buy him a cup of coffee and make sure he feels okay about dating June—your mom, I mean." He paused and looked at me. "You can talk. Get to know Doc better."

"Get to know him better? I've known him since birth!"

"But as your doctor. Not as your mother's, you know .

. . And don't worry. I'll help your mom with the baking until you get back."

I sighed, went around the table, and hugged Matthew. "You're right. This time."

Then I went upstairs to get dressed, leaving him standing in the kitchen.

The Steamy Bean is a quaint little coffee shop on the corner of Red Maple and High Street, across from Village Park on one side and Sugar Tap on the other. It's also just a few steps from the little house Matthew rented, which was, no doubt, why he knew Doc had coffee there every morning. They probably crossed paths frequently on that corner.

"Well, hello, Eloise." Iris Kitchener, owner of the coffee shop, waved at me from the counter.

The Steamy Bean's aesthetic involved walls of exposed, aged brick and warm-stained wood, open shelving, and lots of green plants. It's a cross between cozy and rustic, and always smelled amazing.

Iris was surprised to see me in the morning, because she knew that for me and Mom, that time of the day was usually taken up with baking back at the inn. They say the smells from Pumpkin Hill drift all the way down into the town square when the breeze is out of the west.

"Hi, Iris. Has Doc been in yet?"

"Nope, but he usually arrives right about . . ." She smiled just as the bells above the door jingled and sure enough, Doc walked into the shop, his face down as he tapped away at his cell phone.

"Good morning, Doc," I said as he walked up to the counter. "Can I buy you a drink?"

Doc looked up from his phone, surprised. "Eloise, what brings you here?" He looked down at the time on the phone. "Isn't this baking time up the hill?"

"It is," I said with a nod. "But Mom didn't mind me stepping out for a few minutes. I was hoping to catch you here."

He raised a bushy brow at me, then his face melted into a smile. "Well then, I guess it's our lucky day."

We ordered coffee—which he insisted on paying for despite my protests—and sat at a sunny table at the front of the shop, where we could chat and look out at the park. We stayed for half an hour, and by the time I stood to go, I felt like any ruffled feathers had been smoothed, and Doc knew he and Mom had my wholehearted blessing. In addition to that, Doc's innate bedside manner had left me feeling much calmer about my workload.

"What time is your first appointment today?" I asked him.

"Not until nine," he answered.

"Then how about you walk me home? I know Mom's baking those sour cream scones you love. We can sneak up on her and steal a few."

He laughed and held the door open for me. "You know, Eloise, I think this might be the beginning of a beautiful friendship."

Chapter Four

As Doc and I walked around the square toward home, we got many hellos and a few shouts of "Hey! When are the flatlanders arriving, Eloise?" The whole town was abuzz about the weekend. Every tree branch and lamp post was entwined with twinkle lights, and many of the shop windows were festooned with the murder mystery theme in mind. There was a wonderful display of classic mysteries on offer at the Book Nook. The Black Whale Pub had posted a special mystery-themed menu on their sidewalk chalkboard. Even Suds Gourmet Soap Shop was advertising a *mystery soap box* sale, which turned out to be a small box filled with handmade soaps in the shapes of things like magnifying glasses and footprints. All of this was added to the already amazing fall and Halloween decorations—stacks of pumpkins next to doorways and swags of fall leaves draped around windows. There were jack-o'-lanterns and scarecrows and black cats on display, and the air smelled of dried leaves and coffee and apples, and that crisp, undeniable autumn smell that you only remember when it returns with the first cold front.

Matthew and I had designed the murder mystery weekend to involve any and all of the businesses in town. Our would-be sleuths might question shopkeepers or find clues alongside souvenirs for sale, or mull over their theories at local restaurants while enjoying lunch. Walter had even let me run a few preview articles for the weekend, and the Friday edition of the *Onlooker* would feature a mystery map of the downtown to drum up even more interest. It was going to be an amazing weekend.

After Doc had left to head off to work, his belly full of sour cream scones, and Mom was clearly beaming—and Matthew had given me a quiet nod of approval—it was time to get down to business. A few guests were arriving that morning, but most would get to town the following day, Friday, and we needed to double check that every room was prepped and ready.

"Hello, and welcome," I said cheerily from the front desk as our first couple of guests arrived. I knew these two well. They were Frances and Howard O'Connor, who had come to stay at the inn every October since I was a kid. But the O'Connors were leaf peepers, not amateur detectives. "So glad to see you again, Mr. and Mrs. O'Connor," I said. "Sorry the leaves aren't quite up to snuff this year."

"Oh, you know, climate change," said Howard, taking out a tissue and blowing his nose.

"Good to see you again, Eloise," said Frances. "Gosh, I remember when you were a little girl in pigtails, running around this place with that darling little boy —what was his name?"

"Matthew," I said, smiling. "Mom officially added him to the staff last year. He's around here somewhere."

"How wonderful!"

"Your room is all ready, and I hear there's some beautiful color up Black Bear Mountain."

"What's going on in town?" asked Frances, tilting her

head back in the direction of the square. "It looks even more festive than usual."

"Oh! I'm glad you asked," I said. Then I told them all about the murder mystery event, and they loved the idea.

"How exciting!" said Frances. "There will be a murder right here this weekend!"

Howard cleared his throat, and Frances immediately reddened.

"I mean, but thankfully not a *real* murder this, um, this time," she said.

"No, of course not," I said with a laugh, feeling a few tiny beads of sweat forming on my forehead under my bangs. "And you're both welcome to take a stab at solving the mystery."

"Ooh—is someone getting stabbed?" asked Frances.

I smiled at them and handed over their room keys. "I guess we'll all find out tomorrow!"

Guests continued to trickle in throughout the morning. We actually had to turn a few away since we were already booked for the weekend, but that meant more business for the other inns and hotels around town, which was great for fostering a sense of teamwork in the village.

I stepped out onto our large front porch, now scattered with hay bales and pumpkins—and the faux ravens Matthew was currently fastening to the railing here and there among the swags of fall leaves and sunflowers. Matthew stepped back and looked at the raven he'd been working on, then reached out and adjusted it a tiny bit, then nodded, satisfied.

"Nice touch," I said.

"You don't know the half of it." Matthew gave me a sly smile, pulled a small remote control out of his back pocket, and pressed the button, causing the birds to emit haunting *kraa-kraa* raven calls.

"Wow." I listened carefully. "How did you get the calls to come from the trees, too?"

Matthew paused and listened as the kraa-ing went on. "Oh. Those are real ravens answering these fake ones."

I looked at him. "What are these fake ones saying?

What if the real ones descend on the house to attack the fake ones?"

"That would be awesome."

I rolled my eyes. Matthew and I stood together at the railing and looked down over the village. You could almost feel the excited energy in the air, floating up the hill.

"This is going to be one for the books," said Matthew, slinging an arm around my shoulders.

"Yep," I agreed. "We're going to knock them dead."

Chapter Five

Matthew and I had to get into town to run our last-minute checks-ins with all of our participating businesses. We also had a few props and things to hand out. As the hours of the day were flying by, I could once again feel the stress mounting. I had writing to do for my column and was foreseeing yet another late night. And since the night before hadn't offered much in the way of sleep, that was a problem. If anything, I'd need *extra* energy to make the weekend a success —and there's only so much coffee a person can drink. With Matthew waiting in the inn's jeep, I ran into my cottage to grab a sweater. I stopped by my little bathroom to pull my brown hair back into a high ponytail. I paused and looked at my reflection for a moment.

"So, Miss Smithers . . . What should I do? I love the inn. I love planning fun events like this weekend . . . But I also love writing for the newspaper. I don't want to give either thing up, but I also want to be able to enjoy life, and not always be in a hurry." I leaned closer in. "What's your best advice?" My own brown eyes—with flecks of gold like my father's—looked back at me. I heard the answer inside my head, loud and clear. *Ask for help. Be okay with not being able to do it all—you were never meant to do it all.*

I smiled at my reflection. "Good advice." Then I heard Matthew honking the horn out in the driveway, so I rushed down the stairs and out the door.

Everything was set for the next day, and Mom and I spent the remainder of the afternoon baking up a storm to have delicious breakfast goodies and homemade snacks ready for the weekend.

"I'm going to make a batch of pumpkin pie spice balls," said Mom, opening the large window above the sink to let in some crisp fall air. She inhaled deeply. "I love the smell of autumn. The leaves baking in the sun . . ." She smiled and opened the refrigerator. "Now where is that extra pie?"

"I'll get the chocolate melts," I said, feeling suddenly giddy. I'd made those pumpkin pie spice balls every year with Mom for forever. Every fall, when the air had taken on a little chilly edge, and the leaves were swirling around the hill, and the pumpkins were fresh, we baked up all sorts of pumpkin-based dishes. But the spice balls had always been my favorite, and just the smells of cinnamon and nutmeg woke up the kid who lived in me.

"Are you sure you have time?" Mom asked. She'd taken out the leftover pumpkin pie from our dinner with Doc along with a second pie she'd made that same day that we hadn't even cut into. "Wouldn't you rather take a little time to write?"

I smiled at her. "Nope. I want to make pumpkin pie spice balls with you." I took a large bowl from the cabinet and dumped the pies into it. "I had an epiphany today."

"You did, huh?" Mom handed me the big wooden spoon.

"I can't do it all, Mom. And trying to do it all meant

doing lots of things halfway. Half-heartedly. And it was taking away some of the joy I get out of life. So, I decided to ask for help. I'm going to talk to Walter and step back from a few assignments, and I'm going to really enjoy this weekend at the inn."

Mom smiled. "As long as you know that I support you, even if you choose to leave the inn and focus on your writing."

I stirred the spicy mashed-up pie mixture in the bowl. "I'll never do that. I love the inn too much." I sighed. "I just lost touch with what a blessing it is to welcome guests here and share this place."

Mom and I got to work and before long, we'd whipped up the prettiest batch of pumpkin pie spice balls ever. And we'd talked and laughed while we made them.

Early that evening, I told Mom and Matthew that I was going to run down to Potbelly's and pick up dinner. Mom and Matthew never object to this idea, so were glad to hold down the fort. I had an ulterior motive for going to Edna's restaurant. It had occurred to me earlier in the day that if I needed help with my Miss Smithers column, the ideal person to ask would be the former Miss Smithers. So, I'd asked Walter's permission, and when he'd agreed that I could have Edna spell me whenever the inn was particularly busy, I felt a huge weight lift from my shoulders. Now, if Edna would just agree.

"Well, hello, Eloise," she said, as I entered the restaurant.

"Hi, Edna," I said, breathing in the scents of cream and butter and fresh bread. Edna makes amazing soups, but her breads are equally impressive. I could already smell the yeasty goodness of my favorite honey-butter rolls. "What's hot tonight?"

"I've got a new Hungarian mushroom soup, a chicken tortilla, the coconut curry, and my Vermont cheddar with crispy mini cheese fritters."

"Tough choice, but everyone's nuts about those cheese fritters, so I'll take three of the cheddar to go."

"And extra bread for Matthew," she said with a smile.

As Edna began to ladle out the soup, I gathered my courage and finally asked, "Edna, do you ever miss —" I looked around to see that no one was listening. "Do you ever miss your previous job?"

"You mean"—she lowered her voice to a whisper—"being Miss Smithers?"

I nodded.

Edna thought for a moment. "I suppose I do," she said. "Although I wouldn't want to do it all the time. And you're doing such a fantastic job with the column."

"It's fun." I paused. "But it's a lot to keep up with, especially when things are busy at the inn."

"I can imagine." Edna covered the to-go bowls and began to wrap up three bundles of bread.

"So, I was wondering . . . if you'd ever, say, want to share the column with me—just every now and then." I sighed. "Walter's increasing the number of columns per week, and I'm finding that I need help to keep up with it all. I asked him if it would be okay to ask you to help now and then, and he heartily approved the idea. He said we both do a good job of writing in the Miss Smithers style, so if you're game . . ."

"I *am* game!" Edna said. "This will be great, Eloise! I truly have missed writing for the paper. I just didn't want to commit to doing it all the time. I have other obligations now." She motioned at the cozy restaurant around her.

"That's wonderful! Oh, Edna, I'm so relieved. Can you start this week?"

"Absolutely," Edna said with a resolute nod.

"It would only be for this week, and then I'll let you know when the next time will be."

"You've got yourself a deal." Edna slid a Potbelly's carryout bag across the counter, and I handed her my credit card, feeling elated. Now I would be able to shift all my focus to the Murder in the Haunted Village.

Chapter Six

By the next morning, we were all set to receive the remainder of our guests and get our first-ever murder mystery weekend underway.

"Here they come," I said, nodding at the windows that overlook our front porch and the parking area beyond it.

"Wow. Everyone seems to be arriving in one big clump," said Matthew, cracking his knuckles. He always does that when he's nervous.

"Nothing we can't handle," I assured him.

And I was right. Matthew and I have a system we use for checking guests in when there's a bottleneck situation. I get them registered and he gets their room keys and runs their bulkier luggage up while they're signing on the dotted line. Matthew returns, points them up the stairs, and we move on to the next set of guests. We don't do this all the time, but when we have a crowd—which lately, hasn't been very often—we turn the front desk into a well-oiled machine.

An hour or so after the first guests of the day had arrived, almost all of our rooms were full and people were lounging by the fireplace, drinking hot tea, resting in their rooms, or unpacking and freshening up before the festivities kicked off.

"Well, isn't this quaint?" A tall, thin woman pushed open the front door and stepped inside just as Matthew and I were running over our to-do list. Right on her heels was a short, stout woman. The two had matching beaky noses, designer bags, and high maintenance hair—the tall woman in buttery blond, the short in a sort of chocolate with mauve streaks. They were clearly sisters.

"You must be the Blakes," I said, glancing at my guest list.

"We are! How did you know that?" said the short sister.

"She's clairvoyant," said Matthew, wiggling his eyebrows.

The short sister's eyes widened, and the tall sister raised a skeptical brow. I decided to stick with Matthew's explanation rather than spoil the mystique by admitting they were the last two guests to arrive.

"I'm Carol Blake," said the tall woman. "This is my sister, Stacey."

"We're so glad you're here," I said with my most cordial smile. "Let's get you checked in." I handed Matthew the keys to our finest suite, room seven, and he bolted up the stairs with the sisters' large suitcases.

They watched him go and then turned back to me in unison.

"He's adorable," said Carol.

"And quite strong," added Stacey. "I packed a whole stack of books. That green bag weighs a ton."

"He's pretty handy," I said, giving them a form to fill out. I looked at them a bit more closely for the first time. "You two look familiar. Is there any chance we've met before?"

"Doubtful," said Carol. "This is our first trip to Vermont." She quickly filled out the form, signed it, and slid it back across the counter to me just as Matthew returned.

"Here are your keys, ladies," he said.

"You'll love room seven," I said. "It's at the front of the inn, so it has a glorious view of the village and the mountains beyond. Please let us know if you need anything."

"Thank you," said Carol.

"This may be our best mystery getaway yet," said Stacey.

Carol nodded. "I have a good feeling about it too. But we'll see." She glanced up the stairs, then toward the large family room with its great stone fireplace and smiled. "You know what this reminds me of, Stacey? That little place we stayed during *Semaine Mystère* in Paris."

"Semaine-what?" asked Matthew.

"Oh! It means *Mystery Week*. It was a murder mystery event we recently attended in France," said Stacey.

"Wow," I said. "How exciting!"

"Yes, it was," said Carol. "And the little inn we stayed in was so like this one—*L'auberge Du Fromage*."

I wracked my brain, calling up my two years of high school French. "Fromage? Isn't that cheese?"

"*Oui!*" said Stacey. "On the outskirts of Paris!" (She pronounced it *Paree*, of course.)

"One of the world's oldest cheesemakers was located there—and to this day, they make the most amazing cheeses. But they expanded and now there's an inn as well."

"So, have you done many of these murder mystery events?" asked Matthew.

"Oh yes," said Stacey. "We travel all over the world to solve pretend crimes."

"It's one of our hobbies," said Carol, nodding. "We basically live out of our suitcases."

No pressure there, I thought. I mean, what could an

ancient cheesemaker in the French countryside have on Pumpkin Hill? "Well, we hope you'll have lots of fun this weekend."

"I'm sure we will." Carol slung her very expensive bag over her shoulder and started toward the stairs. "Oh—we have a few more bags in the car." She looked at Matthew. "Would you be a dear—"

"Of course," said Matthew quickly, taking the car keys she held out. "I'll bring them right up."

"I'll help," I said, and the sisters went upstairs while Matthew and I went out to the parking area.

"Thank you," said Carol. "It's the black Mercedes."

"They must be loaded," whispered Matthew, opening the trunk of the gleaming car.

"No kidding," I whispered back.

"Must be nice," he said, taking out the two large tweed suitcases. "To just be able to pick up and travel all over the world, just for fun."

"Yeah, but I'd rather be home," I said. "That probably makes me a stick in the mud."

"No, it does not." Matthew smiled down at me as he closed the trunk.

"Well, they say money can't buy happiness. And those sisters probably have few close friends, other than themselves, since they're always on the go. I would think it would get lonely, traveling all the time." I glanced up at Matthew, who had a funny little smile on his lips. "What?"

"Nothing." He looked down at his shoes. "I was just thinking . . ." He looked back up at me. "I mean, when you said that, I was just thinking how lucky I am that I'm never lonely."

"You're not?"

"Of course not. I have you." The smile left his lips but stayed in his eyes as he looked at me, and heaven help me, I thought my heart would pound out of my chest.

It felt like time had temporarily come to a screeching halt as I stood there in the glorious light of that autumn morning, looking up at Matthew, my oldest and dearest friend—and noticing how incredibly handsome he was, even with his old red baseball cap and his perpetually scruffy hair. He moved a hair closer to me and I found myself unable to move, completely entranced. That was when Carol stepped out onto the front porch.

"Excuse me, but we skipped breakfast this morning," she said, completely oblivious to the bubble of heat she'd just popped. "Is there any chance I could impose upon you? I'm ravenous."

I glanced back at Matthew, who quickly said, "I'll just take these upstairs."

"Come with me to the kitchen," I said, joining Carol on the porch. "We'll whip you up something to tide you over." I held the door open for her and looked back at Matthew one more time, to find him watching, the little smile returning to his lips. He gave a wave, and we went inside.

Chapter Seven

By the afternoon, all of our guests had enjoyed a few fun ice-breaker games and been given a tour of our "haunted" inn during which we told them all about the ghosts that still roamed the streets in town and even the very halls of the inn late at night. They'd also opened their mystery goodie bags, which included things like copies of the latest bestselling cozy mysteries, maps of downtown Williamsbridge, tiny flashlights, small notebooks in which to take notes as they hunted for clues, and brochures of area attractions and local dining and shopping.

The real mystery would get underway over dinner at the Black Whale Pub on the town square, but that wouldn't be until after our late afternoon Sinister

Cocktail Party in the family room, which would allow everyone to get to know each other better. We'd even hired Clay, the bartender from the Black Whale, to mix up all kinds of spooky drinks for our guests. With the French doors open wide, guests could wander out onto the deck and further into the backyard to the fire ring with their drinks and snacks, or mull around the murder board Matthew and I had assembled earlier and discuss their suspicions about what was to come.

With my Miss Smithers duties lifted off my shoulders, I felt a sort of giddy joy. I always get that feeling when autumn arrives, and the leaves change, and the air is crisp. I even took a little extra care with my hair and put on a cinnamon-colored lipstick for the evening, and treated myself to one of Clay's signature cocktails—just one. I chose the frothy white Spider's Web, with its hints of chocolate liqueur, coffee, nutmeg, and sweet whipped cream. Doc Jenkins stopped by—invited by me—and Mom was so pleased to see him that she put away her apron and just enjoyed the party.

I took my cocktail and stood off to one side, next to the cased opening that joins the entry room to the family room, watching our guests mingling and having fun. The mystery wasn't even underway yet, and already the weekend felt like a success. I looked across the smiling faces, listening to the casual banter and laughter. Out in the backyard, several couples had gathered around the fire ring, including the O'Connors, who'd decided to join us after a day of leaf peeping. In the family room, the globetrotting Blake sisters were getting to know Steve and Juliet White, a couple who'd come in from a neighboring town for a romantic weekend getaway, leaving their twelve-year-old son at home with his grandparents.

Matthew came up beside me, a drink in his hand.

"What's that?" I asked, eyeing his florescent green drink, which was served in a laboratory beaker rimmed with what looked like blood red salt crystals.

"Margarita of Death," said Matthew, raising the glass, then taking a sip and shuddering. "Yeah, I can see how this could kill you."

"Mine's amazing," I said, holding up my glass for a toast but then finding it empty. "*Was* amazing."

"Well, I propose a toast anyway," said Matthew, raising his beaker. "To Doc and June." He winked at me and smiled over at Mom and Doc, who were standing together by the fire, chatting with the Blakes and the Whites. "El, I'm proud of you for going to have coffee with Doc, and for inviting him tonight."

"I love Doc," I said. "I just needed a little time to adjust to him being my friend—and Mom's *friend-friend*—instead of just our family doctor." Just then Mom laughed out loud at something. "And Mom sure looks happy these days."

"Love will do that," Matthew said, nudging me.

Before I could come up with a clever response, the front door opened and Leonard Schmidt came in with a young man who looked none too happy to be there.

"Hey, Leonard," Matthew said, setting down his drink and going to shake hands.

"Hello, Matthew."

"How's it going with my pole saw?" Leonard, owner of Leonard's Repair Shop, always had one implement or another of ours on his workbench.

"Got it fixed this afternoon. Had to replace that busted chain. You can pick it up anytime," said Leonard.

"Great. I've got some branches to prune out back. I'll pick it up on my way in on Monday."

Leonard nodded and then seemed to remember the young man next to him. "Oh. This is my nephew, Henry."

The sullen young man looked at Matthew, then me, and gave a nod.

"Welcome, Henry," I said.

"I, uh, was wondering if you have a room available—for Henry here."

"We're pretty well booked for the weekend," I said. "Except for the attic room. It's a cozy little room, but it's very comfortable for only one person." I glanced at Leonard. "Unless you're staying too?" It seemed odd that Leonard would have his nephew to visit and then send him to stay at an inn.

"Oh no, it'll just be Henry," Leonard said quickly. "And his stay is on me." He took out his wallet and handed me his credit card.

"Sure," I said, taking the card. "I'll just run this, and Henry, could I get you to fill out this form?"

Henry sighed and took the form along with a pen from the cup on the desk.

As soon as he slid the form back across the desk to me, Matthew grabbed the key to the attic bedroom from its hook. "Come on, Henry. I'll show you the room. Get you settled in."

"Thanks," Henry said, picking up his small bag. He looked back at his uncle only once, then walked up the stairs behind Matthew.

Leonard looked at me and lowered his voice. "This seems strange, I know. Me putting Henry up here instead of having him at home." He looked up the stairway. "And Henry's none too happy with me for sending him here for the weekend."

"Maybe he'll join in our murder mystery—have a little fun," I said.

"That'd be good," said Leonard, glancing into the family room and pausing, a frown on his face.

"Everything okay?" I asked.

Leonard's eyes stayed glued to the little group gathered around the fireplace.

"Leonard?"

He seemed to snap out of it and turned back to me. "What? Oh. About Henry. He's an unusual young man. He . . . Well, have you ever known one of those people who seems to have trouble following him wherever he goes?"

I nodded.

"That's Henry. And I just think our visit will be nicer if he's not with me round the clock, you know?"

I nodded again. "We'll try to show him a good time whenever he's around the inn."

"Great. Thank you." Leonard seemed content with this. "Ready for the big event tonight?"

"Yep. Are you?"

"All set. Glad my shop is one of the places folks will stop by for clues."

I handed Leonard his receipt. "Thanks for playing along. We'll see you tonight."

"Good. Tell Henry I'll see him soon."

"Will do."

Leonard glanced back into the family room, then turned and left. A few minutes later, Matthew came back downstairs and joined me at the desk.

"Interesting young man," he said. "He said he wanted to stay upstairs and read a while."

"I'll invite him to go with us to the pub for dinner. I have a feeling he needs to stay busy. Leonard said trouble follows him. Not exactly sure what he meant by that, because I didn't want to pry, but I figure if Henry has plenty to do, he'll be less likely to have any time or energy for 'trouble.'"

"Good idea." Matthew looked into the family room. "Everyone seems to be having a great time at the cocktail party." He glanced at his watch. "Half an hour till we gather everyone together and then head into town for dinner."

"Perfect," I said, taking out my phone and checking my email. "Ooh—an email from Rebecca!"

"Rebecca?" Matthew frowned. "Oh, you mean your distant relative, Rebecca?"

"Technically, we're second cousins. Rebecca is my father's cousin's daughter."

"And tell me again why you didn't know about her until recently."

"Because Dad never knew his cousin George Lewis. See, Rebecca and I share the same great grandparents, Martin and Annie Lewis. They had two sons, Robert and William, who didn't get along very well. Robert took his family and moved to Maine, and William stayed in Vermont—right here in this inn where he'd grown up. William had two sons—my father and his brother, who died before he had any children. Meanwhile, Robert had two children, George and Catherine. George had two daughters, one of whom is Rebecca."

"Whew! Family trees." Matthew rolled his eyes.

"No kidding. But before he died, my dad had done some research and had located the Maine branch of the Lewis family. He just never got around to getting in touch with them."

"How old is Rebecca?"

"Twenty-nine. A couple years older than me. And get this—she's also a journalist! Can you believe that?"

Matthew smiled. "It took a lot of courage to reach out to complete strangers. I'm glad you have Rebecca."

"Me too." I clicked off my phone. "But I'll have to write her back later. We have a mystery to get on with. And I do believe that you, my nearly-dearly-departed friend, have a date with the grim reaper."

Chapter Eight

The Black Whale Pub, as usual, smelled amazing. Even if you go there with a full stomach, you'll be hungry the moment you open the door and the smells of Oliver's extra thick burgers and shoestring fries waft out to meet your nose. Oliver Davies owns the Black Whale, and divides his time between the kitchen and the dining areas, where he loves nothing better than greeting guests, telling stories, and shooting the bull. The man has a way with food, and locals and visitors alike always make time to stop in at the Black Whale.

We had ambled down the hill and into town as a group. The cocktail party had been fun and casual, and as far as I could tell, no one had overindulged in the drinks. But one of the great things about living in a walkable town is that you can have a drink and not be faced with the choice of whether or not you ought to drive.

I felt a rush of excitement as Oliver came out to say hello while we were being seated at a long table on the patio off the back of the pub. While the interior of the Black Whale is all warm wood and golden light, with bookshelves stuffed full and a huge old fireplace, the patio at the back is open and airy. Above the tables are wooden beams covered in climbing vines and hung with strings of old fashioned Edison light bulbs that cast a warm glow over the space. Tables are usually scattered all around the patio, and on weekends, there'll be a guitar player in the corner, strumming away, creating a lovely ambience.

Everything looked perfect that night. The patio was scattered with pumpkins, the table set with an eclectic array of jars and vases holding sunflowers and chrysanthemums in fall hues. We all ordered food and drinks and enjoyed a delicious meal.

Just before dessert was served, Matthew quietly slipped away from the table and out the door. I looked up and down at the faces of our guests and smiled.

The O'Connors were chatting with Vernon and Natalie Stokes from Connecticut. Bob and Glenda Fry, in town from New Hampshire, were laughing it up with Juliet and Steve White and the Blake sisters. The only person keeping to himself was Leonard's young nephew, Henry, but for the most part, the ice breaker games and cocktail party had worked their magic. The guests were all at ease with one another, chatting amiably. They hadn't even registered Matthew's absence.

Juliet White erupted in loud laughter at something one of the Blake sisters had said, and then Steve, Juliet's husband, waved the waiter over and ordered another round of drinks for himself and his wife. It occurred to me, as plates of warm apple pie with melting slices of Vermont cheddar were set out in front of everyone, that the Whites might have overindulged a bit. It was apparent by the loud burp that escaped Steve's lips and the way Juliet's eyes had glazed over. I reminded myself that I was hosting a mystery, but not babysitting. These people were all adults. And they were clearly having a good time. I patted myself on the back for encouraging everyone to walk into town rather than drive, and was especially pleased that Henry had decided to join us for dinner and give the evening a chance. I hoped he'd play along with the mystery and made a mental note to try to engage him more. After all, keeping him busy was a surefire way to keep him out of trouble.

When the pie eating was well underway, Oliver came to our table, a worried expression on his face, and whispered something in my ear. I stepped away for a few minutes, but only after raising my voice a bit to tell the person next to me—who happened to be Henry—that I had to take a phone call. (The plan was going like clockwork so far!) When I returned to the table, a look of concern on my face, I picked up my water glass and tapped it with my spoon. Everyone turned expectant and excited eyes toward me.

"I am very sorry to inform you all that our weekend must be cut short—and that you would be wise to hurry back to the inn and pack your bags." I was thrilled to see a few surprised looks from the group. That semester of drama back in middle school was finally paying off. "I certainly can't force you to leave, but I must warn you that if you choose to stay, you do so at your own risk."

"What's going on?" asked Stacey Blake, an edge of anticipation in her voice.

"As you learned earlier today, the Inn at Pumpkin Hill is haunted. And indeed, this whole village is unsafe. In fact, every year around Halloween, when the division between this world and the spirit world seems to dissipate, things begin to happen . . ."

"What?" asked Steve. "What happens?"

"Dark things. *Strange* things. One year, the power went out all over town for no apparent reason. Another year, all of the portraits of past judges that had hung on the courthouse walls fell to the ground, all at once. One time, several families in town, including mine, came home to find their furniture rearranged." I looked around the group and saw that they were paying close attention—even the reluctant Henry. "There have been so many things, I won't even begin to list them all. Books all over the floor at the Book Nook. Lights flashing on and off at Potbelly's Soup Kitchen. Coffee turning bland at the Steamy Bean coffee shop. Missing produce at Whitakers Grocery. Shadows moving through the aisles at the New Leaf Tea House when no one is there. And strange clicking noises at Leonard's Repair Shop. But we here in Williamsbridge, we've always laughed these things off, saying we must be haunted by troublesome spirits. But no serious harm has ever really been done. Until tonight."

"What—what happened?" asked Henry.

"Someone has been murdered," I said slowly.

"Who?" said Carol.

"I'm glad you asked that, Ms. Blake," I said, letting myself smile a little, because frankly, I couldn't help it. "If you will all turn over your dessert plates, you will find a small clue taped to the bottom. Take a few moments now to work together to figure out who has been murdered, and then we'll begin our search for the killer. Because I don't know about you, but I'm not sure whether the killer is some supernatural spirit . . . Or someone who walks here among us."

There was a lot of clinking as people turned over their empty plates and pulled off the little folded notes that had been taped underneath. For the next twenty minutes, they put their heads together, murmuring excitedly amongst themselves. Finally, they looked at me, then looked around.

"Where's Matthew? Is it Matthew?" Stacey yelled.

I nodded slowly with wide eyes.

"According to these clues," Carol called, "the body is very nearby!"

"That's right," said Juliet. "Something about a bridge too far . . . Wait—Williamsbridge! This is Williamsbridge! We crossed a bridge on the way into town!"

"That's right!" said Steve, thrusting a finger into the air. "Let's go!"

Chairs were shoved back, bills were paid, and we all left the Black Whale and trotted down Sugar Maple Street to William's Bridge. It was getting dark by then, so people took out flashlights and looked all around the bridge. There was an excited shriek of horror when one of the ladies spotted the deceased Matthew, sprawled on the grassy ground beside Cottontail Creek, just behind the Duck and Pheasant, Williamsbridge's swankiest restaurant.

We all rushed over, and right on cue, our local law enforcement duo, Detective Phil Dunlap and Officer Marvin Potts hurried out of the shadows.

"What's going on here?" asked Dunlap.

"Look, sir! It's Matthew Stewart, from the inn!"

Officer Potts knelt next to the motionless Matthew and took his pulse. "And he's dead!"

There was another shriek, this time from Howard O'Connor, who looked to be having the time of his life. This was followed by animated chatter, as people whipped out their cell phone cameras, clue notebooks, and pens. A careful examination by Dunlap and Potts revealed that Matthew (gasp!) had been poisoned!

I had an extremely hard time holding in the laughter that was threatening to burst forth as I acted distressed and watched Matthew trying to stay 'dead.' It was tempting to let Dunlap and Potts go on and on pointing out the reasons they'd deduced that it was poison that had killed him, just to see if he'd crack.

"Look! What's this?" Henry, who had stepped shyly aside spoke up. He was standing nearby, but further down the sloping ground toward the creek.

Everyone looked up and walked to where Henry stood pointing at a half-empty to-go coffee cup that lay spilled on the ground.

"Maybe it was his!" said Henry.

"Well done, detective," said Dunlap, squatting down next to the overturned cup.

"Sharp eyes," agreed Potts, his own eyes narrowing as he nodded shrewdly.

"It's a cup from the Steamy Bean!" said Stacey. "Maybe the poison was in Matthew's drink."

"We'll send this off to the lab," said Dunlap.

"And I'll call the ambulance to come and take poor old Matthew away," I said, dabbing my eyes with a tissue.

Then I reached into my trusty backpack and took out a stack of envelopes, each with the name of a different guest written across the front. "Meanwhile," I said, passing out the envelopes, "if there's any justice in this world, we must find Matthew's killer. It's up to you all to figure out who committed this heinous crime. Because I have the feeling it wasn't our neighborhood ghost . . . Or was it?"

The would-be detectives anxiously ripped open their envelopes and began reading their clues.

"You'll have to walk all over town to question the locals about what they've seen and heard. Start compiling your clues, and then later, we'll head back up the hill to work on our murder board. Tomorrow, there will be more clues. I just hope you can find the killer before anyone else ends up"—I looked down at Matthew—"like *this* poor, pitiful man."

There was an excited hum of conversation as people mulled over their clues. I walked along with them to High Street, glancing back only once at Matthew who, still lying on the ground, gave me a thumbs up.

Chapter Nine

❦

The whole town square looked beautiful. There's something magical about Williamsbridge at night. The maple trees that line the streets glisten with little white lights. Shop windows are warmly lit from within, and restaurants keep a steady stream of customers walking up and down the sidewalks. The cozy lantern lights all around Picadillee Park come on, lighting the various pathways that wind around among the trees.

Matthew and I had hidden clues in the park, and given instructions to every participating shop and restaurant owner. The participants' clues would take them in different directions, but if all went according to plan, they would be able to return to the inn and create the murder board, putting all of their clues together to begin drawing conclusions about who would have a motive to kill Matthew. Then on Saturday after a hearty breakfast, they would need to find the proof and locate the killer, at which time Dunlap and Potts would return for their encore performance and arrest the culprit. Then Saturday evening would be a fun "debriefing dinner" at the Duck and Pheasant, and Sunday would be a free day, with optional visits to Sugar Tap, coffee at the Steamy Bean, a visit with a few local Vermont mystery authors at the Book Nook, shopping around the square, and a hike around Black Bear Mountain.

The group began to disperse—beginning with Carol and Stacey, who ran off giggling after opening their clue envelopes. Within a few moments, everyone had gone off in different directions, mostly in sets of two, leaving Henry and me standing alone on the sidewalk.

"I'm glad you decided to join in tonight," I said.

"This is fun," he admitted. "I've never done anything like this before." He shifted from foot to foot. "But now . . . I'm not sure. Maybe I should just go back up to the inn."

"Why? The fun's just getting started."

"Well, it's just . . . everyone else came to the inn with someone. And since Uncle Leonard deserted me, I'm the only one who's on my own." He glanced at me. "I don't guess you'd consider walking around town with me, so I don't look like a complete dork."

I smiled. "I don't see what harm there could be in that. I won't help you, I'll just keep you company."

He looked relieved. "That would be great. Thanks."

"So," I nodded at the envelope he still hadn't opened, "what's your first clue?"

Henry opened his envelope. "Speak of the devil. It says I need to go and question Uncle Leonard at his repair shop."

I lowered my voice. "Now you know why he couldn't hang out with you tonight. He's part of the mystery."

That seemed to make Henry feel a little better.

"Let's go," I said, setting off down the sidewalk.

Henry jogged to catch up with me, clearly in a much lighter mood now.

"Hey, that's not fair!" Steve, who was walking in the opposite direction with Julia pointed at Henry and me. It was pretty clear by the way he wobbled that he'd definitely had too much to drink at dinner.

"Steve, don't be such a baby," Julia scolded, scoffing at her husband.

"Well, it's true," said Steve. "She's the one who created this whole murder mystery. She already knows who the killer is. If she helps him, it isn't fair."

"You really are vile sometimes, Steve," said Julia, who also seemed to have let down her polite guard as a result of tying on one too many.

"No worries," I said, holding up a hand. "Henry here was just walking me as far as Potbelly's. I'm running in there to chat with my friend Edna." I looked at Henry and gave him a secret wink.

Steve seemed satisfied with this. "Okay. Well. Sorry."

"Let's go," said Julia, taking Steve's arm. "We're falling behind." They crossed the street and disappeared into the Book Nook.

"Now what?" asked Henry, looking frustrated. "If you come with me, they might see from the windows of the bookstore. And I wouldn't put it past that Steve guy to be watching us right this second."

"How about this," I offered. "I'll go into Potbelly's for a few minutes. You head on to Leonard's Repair Shop. I'll stroll that way shortly. We can go on from there together. We'll just keep our eyes peeled for Steve and Julia."

"Good idea," said Henry. "See you later." He waved goodbye and walked on down High Street, and I went into Potbelly's.

As it turned out, Edna wasn't there at the moment, so I popped right back out and headed casually down High Street, taking a right on Red Maple and crossing William's Other Bridge. Yes, our town founder—after building our iconic bridge over Cottontail Creek, built a second bridge further down the creek and the name stuck. The road became more shadowy as I got further from the square, and the night got quieter. Henry couldn't be far ahead, but I didn't see him. I could hear the sounds of crickets chirping and the occasional call of one great horned owl to another from the woods toward Gunther Hill. The wind blew, whistling through the trees and rustling fallen leaves.

If Matthew had been with me, I would've thought it was a beautiful, peaceful night. But all alone, and with thoughts of murder at the front of my mind, I felt suddenly spooked. I picked up my pace, and felt a wave of relief when I saw Leonard's Repair Shop just ahead on the left. The front door was slightly ajar, and light from inside poured out onto the sidewalk. As I hurried up the path, I jumped at the sight of something small stooping in the shadows of the flower bed to the right of the door. I whipped out my flashlight and laughed at myself when I saw that it was just a garden gnome with plump, rosy cheeks, smiling away.

"Of course, *you're* not spooked," I whispered to the gnome. "Gnomes are never spooked."

"There you are!"

I almost jumped out of my skin a second time as Henry emerged from the darkness to the other side of the door. I spun around. "Henry!" I caught my breath. "You scared me half to death. Where were you?"

"Right over there, leaning against the wall."

"Why didn't you say anything when I walked up? Or go on inside to see your uncle?"

Henry looked embarrassed. "First, could you not shine your flashlight directly into my eyes?"

"Oh. Sorry." I stuffed the flashlight into my backpack.

"I just got here. And since things aren't great between me and Uncle Leonard right now, I decided to wait for you. And I didn't say anything as you walked up because I was considering jumping out and startling you . . . which I now see might not have been the best idea."

I laughed, lightening the mood. "You're just lucky I didn't whack you with my karate chop."

He laughed as well, and I pushed open the front door the rest of the way. The first thing that caught my attention was the tidiness of the place. Large squares of pegboard hung on the walls, and little hooks supported all manner of tools as well as little rows of jars, each neatly labeled with the name of its contents. The shelves were lined with larger items and boxes, everything labeled and in its place. A huge work island took up the center of the room, and I smiled as I noticed Matthew's pole saw lying across it, ready for pickup.

"Where is he?" Henry's voice snapped me out of my

momentary reverie about getting Leonard to help us organize the shop at the inn.

I looked around. "He should be here. He's part of our mystery."

Henry looked around too. "Well, he doesn't seem to be." Outside, the wind whistled, causing the front door to blow shut with a loud slam. Henry and I both jumped this time. "Let's just go," he said nervously.

"But you'll need him to guide you to the next clue. Let's give Leonard a few more minutes. Maybe he just stepped out."

Henry nodded and walked around to the other side of the island, then stopped dead in his tracks. "Oh no."

"What is it?"

When Henry didn't move and didn't answer, I walked slowly around the island, a sudden sense of foreboding sending a chill up and down my spine.

Leonard was lying on the floor. I automatically rushed over to him and felt for a pulse, but then noticed his open, glassy eyes. I jumped back, horrified.

"Hurry! Dial 9-1-1!" I wasn't actually talking to

Henry, who still stood there frozen in shock. I was talking to myself, which I tend to do when I get nervous. I dug in my backpack, found my phone, made the call, and was told the police and ambulance were on the way.

"Come on," I said, pulling Henry toward the door by the arm. "Let's wait outside."

"I, uh, okay." Henry looked ten shades of pale. I took him out front and had him sit down on a bench, then sat down next to him, feeling a little dizzy myself.

Then I texted Matthew, who was hiding out at the little house he rents on High Street, just off the square —since he was supposed to be dead. He didn't text back, but instead must've flown to his truck and driven over to Leonard's, because he got there before the ambulance.

I felt my jaw unclench when I saw Matthew running toward Henry and me. I jumped up and ran into his arms. I would've stayed there longer, but we were accosted by flashing lights and sirens.

What followed was a blur. Doc rode over in the ambulance, as he sometimes does, and our two paramedics, Maude and Larry, rushed into Leonard's shop with their stretcher. Officer Potts and Detective Dunlap questioned me and Henry separately about what we'd seen and whether we'd noticed anything strange. I was glad that Henry hadn't gone into the repair shop before I'd arrived there. At least he hadn't been alone when he'd found his uncle dead. When Potts was done questioning me, he walked over to confer with Doc, who was standing outside the shop, writing something on a clipboard as the paramedics carried Leonard's body to the waiting ambulance.

"Looks like a blow to the head with a blunt object," Doc said to Potts. "We'll know more when we get him to the coroner."

Doc left Potts and walked over to me. "Are you okay, Eloise?"

I nodded, paused, and then shook my head. "Not really."

Doc looked at Matthew. "You should get her home."

Matthew took my hand and started to move toward his truck.

"Wait. We have to wait for poor Henry," I said.

Henry was still talking to Dunlap, so Matthew and I stood off to one side and waited.

"What were you and Henry even doing here anyway?" Matthew whispered.

"What do you mean? We were following Henry's clue. It said to come here and talk to Leonard."

"But that wasn't the clue I put into Henry's envelope," said Matthew. "That was in one of the White's—either Steve or Julia's."

"Are you sure?"

"Yep."

"What are we going to do? We can't just go on with the weekend like nothing's happened."

Matthew let out a long sigh. "I think we have to cancel the event. Offer people the option to stay in town and enjoy themselves or go home. I just don't see how we can run a mystery game when a man has died."

"You're right." I felt deflated and disappointed and sad all at once.

"Don't you think this is strange though—this thing with Henry?"

"What thing with Henry?" I glanced over at Henry, who was still deep in conversation with Potts and Dunlap.

"Well, he shows up in town for a visit, his own uncle puts him up at the inn, then he mistakenly gets the Leonard clue . . . and now Leonard's dead."

"But Henry didn't kill Leonard," I said.

"You sound pretty sure of that."

"I am. I mean, you should've seen how shocked he was when he saw Leonard. And besides, he was still outside the shop when I arrived, and he was only out of my sight for a few minutes."

"How long does it take to whack someone over the head?"

Chapter Ten

We didn't end up bringing Henry home with us, because Dunlap and Potts took him to the station for further questioning. He was, after all, Leonard's relative and had been the one to find the body. The poor kid looked exhausted and wan.

Once we'd contacted all the other guests and rounded everyone back up at the inn, all heck broke loose. The group was divided three ways: There were the people who had been having a ball downtown and wanted to keep hunting for clues and interrogating witnesses and suspects. There were those who thought we should take the rest of the evening off and then regroup and resume the mystery the next day. And then there were those who were genuinely horrified that a person had been brutally murdered along the mystery route—and that they might have just as easily been the ones to discover the body.

"I don't see why we shouldn't go on with the weekend," said Stacey Blake. "It's not like we can all postpone and come back to Vermont two weeks from now. By then, Carol and I will be in Bavaria, for crying out loud!"

"But a person has *died*—a person who is related to that guy over there," said Bob Fry, lifting his chin toward Henry, who was just coming through the door.

I hurried up to him and asked him if I could do anything for him, but he just shook his head and trudged upstairs.

Once Henry was safely away, Bob's wife Glenda nodded in agreement with her husband. "And he didn't just die. He was *murdered*. As far as we know, no one has been arrested at this point. And that means there's a killer on the loose out there somewhere in the dark!"

"Could be a raving lunatic," agreed Vernon Stokes. "A madman. Ooh—a serial killer!"

"Well, I think we can all agree on one thing: if we don't solve a murder, we should all get a full refund," said Carol.

At this pronouncement, there were general murmurings of agreement from the group.

"Oh great. That's the one thing they all agree on." I looked at Matthew, panicked.

He and I both knew the expense, the investment of both time and money, we'd already made on behalf of the inn for the weekend. And with the way business had slowed down lately and with the fall color not drawing as many leaf peepers this year, we couldn't afford to take the kind of hit that giving full refunds to everyone would entail—not to mention the loss of business for the rest of the town.

I felt like I was being pressed between a rock and a hard place. I didn't want to be a jerk and just go on with the weekend. Leonard had been an integral part of our mystery. And the thought of just proceeding as though nothing had happened didn't jibe with my conscience—and that feeling was sharpened every time I thought about Henry, who had just lost his uncle.

On the other hand, we were all counting on this first murder mystery weekend being a success—and that feeling was sharpened every time I looked over at my mom, who was bustling around serving cookies and cocoa, trying to make people comfortable.

I looked at Matthew again, and he must've seen the desperation in my eyes, because he said, "What if we solved a real murder mystery instead?"

"What?" Stacey, who was standing nearest to Matthew perked up.

"Oh—sorry, I was just thinking out loud," said Matthew.

"No, that's a brilliant idea!" said Stacey.

"What's a brilliant idea?" asked Carol, her sharp voice causing the chatter in the room to instantly die down.

"We solve a *real* murder mystery," said Stacey. "The case of *who killed Leonard the repairman*! We've never solved an *actual* murder before."

There was a moment of complete silence followed by a renewal of the excited chitchat. The consensus was most definitely in favor of staying on and trying to figure out who killed Leonard.

"This is crazy," I whispered to Matthew.

"Is it, though?" he wondered. "This way, we keep all of these people in Williamsbridge for the weekend. They are occupied and happy. And we don't owe everyone their money back. Plus, we honor Leonard's memory by helping to bring his killer to justice."

He was right.

Stacey drew a little cartoon sketch of Leonard and pinned it to the middle of the murder board. "This is going to be the thrill of a lifetime," she said. "Let's solve this mystery!"

The rest of the group clapped and gathered around, talking about where to start with their investigation. I realized as I watched them, that the weekend had just, bizarrely enough, become quite simple from the innkeeping perspective. Mom, Matthew, and I would no longer be in charge of entertaining anyone. All we'd do would be to offer breakfast and snacks and warm drinks in the evenings.

I stepped into the kitchen where I ducked into the pantry and called Edna. "Good news, Edna. I can write the Miss Smithers column this weekend after all."

"Too late," Edna said, and I could hear the smile in her voice. "I already wrote the next three. There were so many great questions in the pile! I forgot how much fun it was to answer them. I've missed being Miss Smithers, truth be told."

I sighed.

"What is it?" Edna asked.

"It just occurred to me that maybe I should give you back the column. I love writing it, but it takes a lot of time. And running the inn is so demanding. I don't want to be harried and stressed all the time. And now, with poor Leonard being murdered . . ."

"I heard," said Edna. "Poor Leonard."

"And it's yet another murder connected to the inn. If this goes on, no one will want to come and stay here ever again. I'm afraid our reputation will take another hit and people will start calling us the Inn at Murder Hill." I sighed. "Edna, I'm mortified."

"Now listen to me," said Edna, the sweet calm of her

voice a soothing balm to my nerves. "You worry too much. The column is covered for the week. We'll put our heads together and figure out how to handle it going forward later. For now, you take Miss Smithers' advice. Take a deep breath and let go of those worries. All will be well."

Matthew suddenly stuck his head into the pantry. "Here you are. I've been looking all over."

"Edna, thank you," I said. "I'll talk to you later. Duty calls."

Chapter Eleven

I wasn't sure how late our guests had stayed up Friday night, because somewhere after midnight, I conked out with my head on the table. There was probably drool involved. Matthew jiggled me awake and walked me out to my cottage, then headed home. At that point, our amateur sleuths were still going strong, starting on a fresh pot of coffee and planning their investigation.

Saturday morning, I was in the middle of a dream in which Matthew was trimming a huge tree branch with a pole saw which suddenly went up in flames, and then the tree was falling, and just before Matthew got squished, I woke up, sat upright in bed, and tried to take deep breaths to get my heart rate to settle.

Once I'd calmed down, I looked at the clock. It was already seven-thirty! I'd fallen into bed without setting my alarm the night before. I rushed into the bathroom and splashed my face with cold water, chiding myself for being the only person left in the world who still used an old fashioned alarm clock. I went for the messy-bun look, since that was the best I could do in the shortest amount of time, and ran over to the main house, where Mom was already pulling a tray of cinnamon rolls out of the oven.

"I'm so sorry, Mom," I said, realizing just then that she was glowing in that way she had been lately. I smiled at her. "Thinking of Doc?"

"Why would you say that?"

"Just a guess."

"I just love cinnamon rolls. Don't you?"

"Mom, you know I do." I rolled my eyes and gave her a playful nudge.

Frankly, Mom's cinnamon rolls right out of the oven are almost as good as being in love. But the cream cheese frosting puts them over the top. She gave a big bowl of the creamy frosting a stir and put a generous pat over each hot roll. This way, the frosting could melt down into every crack and crevice. Then, once they've cooled a little, Mom's trick is to put a *second* dollop of frosting on each roll, which gets swirled around and looks beautiful.

"Don't worry about oversleeping," said Mom. "No one's come down yet anyway."

"Probably because they just went to bed a few hours ago," I said with a laugh. "I'm glad they're sleeping in."

I ground up coffee beans and filled a pitcher with orange juice, then went into the dining area and prepped the big stainless steel coffee urn. I figured everyone would need an extra cup to get them going this morning. I glanced toward the other end of the large room—the family room end. I walked over to clear the ashes out of the fireplace and reset it for that evening. Then the murder board caught my eye.

The cartoon Leonard was tacked into the middle. There was a list of assignments for each person to undertake that day. And at the top, in bold letters, was a list of motives. *Revenge. Greed. Passion. Theft gone wrong.* Then, at the bottom of the list in smaller handwriting was scrawled, *Killer might just be a raving lunatic.* Clearly that would have to be Vernon's contribution.

Stacey trotted into the room, looking entirely too bright-eyed for someone who'd been up almost all night. "Good morning," she said cheerily.

"Good morning," I said, turning away from the murder clue board. "How are you today?"

"Great. I didn't sleep a wink, but I'm great," said Stacey. She looked at the board. "What do you think?"

"Looks to me like you've already made some great progress," I said.

"I have another clue." Stacey looked around and lowered her voice. "But I can't put it on the board where everyone can see it."

"Really?"

She nodded slowly.

"Could you tell me what it is?"

She stepped a little closer. "It's about Steve and Juliet."

"The Whites? What about them?" I glanced toward the staircase and saw that no one was coming down. "I promise I won't tell."

"They're in the room next to ours. And this morning, while Carol was in the bathroom, I heard them having a terrible fight." She looked around, wide-eyed, one more time and whispered, "Juliet said something about the blood on Steve's clothes, and Steve said 'What blood? I don't know what you're talking about.'"

Just then, we heard someone coming down the stairs and stepped apart, doing our best to look like we'd been talking about nothing more interesting than the weather. Thankfully, it was Carol who entered the room. She hurried over to us.

"Stacey, you ran out before I'd finished my makeup. Did you hear—" She stopped talking abruptly and glanced at me.

"It's okay," Stacey said quietly. "Eloise knows. I told her."

Carol nodded. "Something's going on there."

"So how did Steve White get blood on his clothes?" wondered Stacey.

"Maybe from the bloody nose he had yesterday," whispered Carol, as if she were divulging a scandalous secret. "Didn't you notice?"

Stacey and I looked at each other.

"I didn't," I said.

"But now that you mention it, I did notice a little dried blood at the edge of one of his nostrils," said Stacey.

"Maybe he just gets nosebleeds," I suggested. "Matthew gets them now and then, especially when the air is dry."

"This wasn't that kind of nosebleed," said Carol, crossing her arms over her chest. "A bruise was forming under his left eye."

"I thought he had circles under his eyes. I just figured he was tired," said Stacey.

"Nope. That was the beginning of a bruise. Not a bad one—and not one you'd really notice if you weren't looking for it. I figure Steve got punched in the nose yesterday afternoon, and did a good job cleaning himself up." Carol looked at her perfectly manicured nails. "Anyway, maybe that's where the blood on his shirt came from."

"But why would he lie about it to his wife?" Stacey asked.

Carol shrugged. We all stood silently, pondering and looking at the clue board. Then we heard footsteps once again coming down the wooden staircase, and I thanked the heavens above that those stairs squeaked so horribly—a feature I hadn't loved as a teen. No one could sneak up or down the stairs at our house.

"Thanks for telling me this," I whispered to the Blake sisters. Then I raised my voice to a normal volume and said, "There's coffee in the urn over there, and I'll go bring out Mom's amazing cinnamon rolls."

I hurried off to the kitchen, where Matthew was just coming in through the back door.

"Coffee," he groaned.

I poured him a cup from the kitchen pot, then poured a cup for myself and sat down at the table. Mom bustled into the dining room with a big platter piled high with eggs and bacon.

"When did we get old?" Matthew asked. "We used to be able to stay up late and still feel fine the next day."

"Tell me about it."

"You sound like an old married couple," said Mom, who'd come back into the kitchen.

I felt my cheeks getting warm at her remark. "What's gotten into you Mom? You're cooking up a storm today."

"It's called eight hours of sleep," Mom said, stirring a pan of sizzling hash browns on the stovetop.

"Don't rub it in," I said, getting up to dig through the drawer for headache medicine.

When Mom left the kitchen again, I sat back down in the chair next to Matthew's. "We need to talk."

He raised a brow over the rim of his mug. "What did I do?"

I swatted his arm. "You're not in trouble, goofy. I need to tell you what the Blake sisters just told me."

I filled him in on how Stacey and Carol had heard Steve and Juliet fighting in their room, about the mention of blood on Steve's shirt, and the bloody nose.

"Who punched Steve, I wonder," said Matthew.

"That's the question," I said. "Clearly it wasn't his wife, because she was asking him about the blood and he was denying anything had happened."

"Which means he was lying to his wife," added Matthew. "But they're from out of town. Who does Steve know here to even get into a fight with? I mean, surely he didn't get punched by some complete stranger."

"The Blakes live less than an hour from here. So, it's not that unlikely that they know local people."

Matthew sighed. "Maybe this will make sense after another cup of coffee."

Mom, who had hurried into the dining area with a plate of hash browns came back into the kitchen and took a tray of blueberry muffins out of the oven.

"Mom, what has gotten into you? You're like a machine today!"

"Just getting ahead a bit," said Mom. "I'll wrap these up and we can serve them tomorrow. I'll go check on the coffee."

"Mom, let me help you."

"No, you just sit," she said, going back into the dining area and taking the cinnamon rolls with her.

I turned back to Matthew. "We need to do a little investigating ourselves. And I think we should start by checking in with Henry. He said he and his uncle weren't getting along—"

"Well clearly," said Matthew. "Otherwise, surely Leonard would've invited Henry to stay at his house."

"Exactly. I'd like to know what caused the rift between those two."

Matthew stood and pushed the swinging kitchen door open a crack, peering in at the guests. "Henry's not at breakfast yet," he said, coming back to the table.

"Let's go up and check his room. Make sure he's okay."

"El, we're not busting into his room," said Matthew.

"Of course not! We'll just loiter in the hall a little,

maybe knock softly." I looked at the clock. "It's ten-thirty, Matthew. Surely he's awake by now. And after the trauma of last night, I just feel like we should check on him."

Matthew begrudgingly agreed, and we went into the dining area.

"Where are you two off to?" asked Mom as we passed through the room.

"We're just running upstairs to check in with Henry," I said. "He looked pretty shaken up when he got back from the police station last night."

"Don't bother," said Mom. "He's checked out."

"What?" I looked at her, confused. "He was supposed to stay through the weekend. When did he leave?"

"I'm not sure," said Mom with a little shrug. "I didn't see him leave. But I took a load of fresh towels upstairs early this morning, and his door was standing wide open. I peeked inside and all of his things were gone."

"Well, that's a little suspicious, don't you think?" said Steve, who was filling his plate at the sideboard. "For Henry to run away like that?"

"We'd better put this on the clue board," said Stacey, hurrying into the family room.

"Definitely," agreed Steve. The whole group followed Stacey, while Matthew and I hung back with Mom.

"I can't believe this," I said. "He didn't even say goodbye? Just left?"

"Well, he did leave a note," said Mom. "I have it in the kitchen, on my desk."

Matthew and I looked at each other.

"Mom, we need to see that note."

Chapter Twelve

The viewing of the note Henry had left behind was a bit anticlimactic. In small, tidy script, it simply read, *I'm checking out early, but don't want to wake anyone. The murder mystery was fun. Thanks.*

"So that's that," I said, folding the note in half. "He's really gone."

"Maybe Steve and Stacey had a point," said Matthew. "It is a little suspicious."

We heard a bit of commotion in the family room and returned there to find Detective Dunlap and Officer Potts had arrived.

"We're here to take statements from each of you," said Dunlap, hands resting on his belt.

"We thought it would be more convenient if we came to you, rather than asking you all to come down to the station," added Potts.

Mom and I shook our heads. Dunlap and Potts would generally think of any excuse to do their questioning at the inn. They both had a weakness for Mom's baked goods and knew she was too good a host not to offer up something tasty.

"Why question us?" asked Julia. "We weren't the ones who found the body."

"Just a bit of a formality," explained Dunlap. "We thought we'd talk to everyone who was involved in the murder mystery."

"The Williamsbridge PD leaves no stone unturned," said Potts. "We told, uh," Potts glanced at his notepad, "Henry Schmidt, the deceased's nephew, that we'd follow up with him this morning, so we'll start with him."

"There may be a problem there," I said. "Henry checked out."

"He did *what?*" said Dunlap. "We specifically told him to stay put."

"We didn't even know he'd gone," I explained. "He left this note. He must've headed out either late last night or very early this morning."

Dunlap took the note and read it, Potts peering over his shoulder.

"Did any of you see him leave?" Dunlap asked the group.

All of them shook their heads solemnly.

"Want me to put out an APB, boss?" asked Potts.

Dunlap thought a moment. "Not yet. I'm sure we can track him down if we need him." He looked at the faces of our guests. "Are all the rest of you here, or is anyone else missing?"

"This is everyone," I said. "We had fifteen guests before Henry left, and there are fourteen here."

Dunlap nodded. "This shouldn't take long, folks. Officer Potts will speak to half of you. I'll speak to the other half." He looked at me, Mom, and Matthew. "We'll talk to you three before we leave."

Mom smiled. "Of course. Coffee?"

Dunlap brightened. "Thank you, June. That would be great."

"Something sure smells good," Potts hinted.

"I've got a fresh batch of muffins. I'll bring some in," said Mom.

While the local law enforcement duo got down to business, Matthew and I got our own investigation underway.

"Let's check Henry's room," I whispered, and Matthew nodded. We slipped out of the family room and up the stairs.

"We have to hurry. Dunlap and Potts aren't going to want anyone up here," I said, peering into Henry's room and sweeping around it with my eyes. Nothing looked to be amiss. Henry's bed had been slept in. The drawers and closet were empty.

"Darn," said Matthew. "What now?"

"Let's take a look at Henry's check-in form. He should've listed his next of kin. Maybe we can at least check with whoever that is and make sure he's okay."

We snuck down the stairs, avoiding the attention of Dunlap and Potts, and went to the front room. I took out Henry's form and found a Richard Schmidt listed as Henry's father. "Jackpot!" I said.

"Must be Leonard's brother. Call him," urged Matthew.

I dialed the number, and a man answered on the third ring.

"Yello," he said.

"Oh—hi, Mr. Schmidt?" I said.

"Yep, that's me."

"Hello." I suddenly felt as awkward as my twelve-year-old self. "This is Eloise Lewis. I'm calling from the Inn at Pumpkin Hill in Williamsbridge."

There was a confused pause. "Yes?"

"Your son, Henry, was our guest last night."

"He was? So, Leonard didn't have the decency to put him up?" Richard scoffed. "Might've guessed."

"Leonard is, uh, was your brother, I assume?"

Another pause.

Did Richard not know that his brother was dead? "I'm very, very sorry to have to tell you this, Mr. Schmidt, but Leonard is no longer . . . well, he died."

I felt my throat go dry and looked at Matthew, who had been leaning his ear next to the phone so he could hear the conversation. He motioned for me to go on.

"I'm so sorry for your loss," I said.

"I heard from a police officer there this morning," said Richard. "Truth is, my brother and I hadn't spoken for years." He sighed. "I've been trying to reach Henry, but haven't gotten through. I figured he was still over at Leonard's. Or with the police. Is he there at the inn, then?"

"Well, that's the thing," I said. "Henry left without checking out. Nobody saw him go. I was worried about him, and was calling you to check on him. I guess he's not home yet?"

"I'm only forty-five minutes away. When did he leave?" Richard's voice was becoming more concerned by the second.

"I don't know for sure, but it was longer than forty-five minutes ago. He was gone early this morning. He left a note."

"A note? Henry?" There was a long pause. "That doesn't sound like him at all. None of this sounds right. I'd like to see that note. I'll get in my car and head your way now."

I quickly stopped him. "But then if Henry gets home, you won't be there. Let me text you a photo of the note. You can read it for yourself."

Matthew nodded and jogged into the family room, returning with the note almost immediately.

"I'm impressed," I whispered to him. "That was very stealthy of you."

"Dunlap had left it sitting on the sideboard next to the coffee," Matthew said with a snicker.

I snapped a picture of the note and Matthew ran it back into the dining area. I sent the photo to Richard. There was a pause while he looked at it.

"Henry didn't write that," he said, bringing the phone back up to his ear. "No way."

"How can you be so sure?" I asked.

"It's not his handwriting for starters. And Henry has dyslexia. He gets his b's and d's mixed up. The ones in this note are all perfect."

I looked down at the check-in form I'd watched Henry fill out the day before. Sure enough, the handwriting was looser and sloppier, and in several instances a *b* replaced a *d*, and vice versa. I looked at Matthew, who looked as shocked as I felt.

"Mr. Schmidt—"

"Call me Richard. Please."

"Richard, why do you think Henry would leave the inn so abruptly?"

"Because he's afraid," said Richard. "When the police called me this morning, they informed me that they'd tried questioning him last night, but that Henry was overwrought and exhausted, so they were going to be questioning him more extensively today. I talked to Henry briefly last night, but he just wanted to go to sleep. Didn't even tell me he wasn't at Leonard's house, where I assumed he'd be. Knowing Henry, he thinks the police want to talk to him more because they suspect that he killed Leonard." He sighed. "Henry wouldn't hurt a fly. He only went to

Williamsbridge because he loves the fall leaves and wanted to hike around Black Bear Mountain. The boy is an avid leaf peeper. He gets so frustrated with himself with his learning issues. But he loves to be out in nature. I told him I didn't recommend going to stay with Leonard. But he was determined."

"So, you and Leonard . . . You said you hadn't spoken in years? What happened?"

When Richard didn't answer right away, I knew I'd pushed it too far. I'd gone from concerned innkeeper to prying buttinsky in one second flat.

"Let's just say we had a difference of opinion that ran pretty deep. It concerned our moral values," Richard finally said.

"Sorry, I didn't mean to intrude."

"That's okay."

"Well, now that Henry's left in such a hurry, the police are going to be looking for him," I said, taking a peek into the family room, where Stacey and Carol appeared to be attempting to explain the murder clue board to Dunlap and Potts. "I suspect you'll be hearing from them soon."

"I don't doubt it," said Richard. "But right now, all I care about is finding my son."

After hanging up with Richard, I tucked Henry's check-in form back into my files.

"So, where his Henry?" Matthew wondered.

I shook my head, feeling more confused than ever. "And who wrote that note?"

Chapter Thirteen

The rest of Saturday was a blur of our guests coming and going from town, bringing clues to pin to the murder board. I studied the board a few times when no one was around, but couldn't make much sense of it. They seemed to suspect that the culprit was either Maude from Suds Gourmet Soaps, or Ed from Ed's Pop and Shop—neither of whom would've had any motive to kill Leonard in my estimation. Nevertheless, I was grateful that our guests were clearly having fun and not doing anyone any harm. There was still palpable tension between Steve and Julia White, but it wasn't until Sunday morning that I found out just how deep their issues were.

Steve came downstairs early in the morning. I was

already at work at the front desk, updating a few things on the computer.

"I'd like to request a different room for tonight," said Steve, who looked like he'd been up all night.

"For you and your wife? Is there a problem with your room?" I asked. They were staying in one of our most charming suites, so I was surprised by his request.

Steve looked around as though checking that no one else was nearby. "Just for me."

"Oh. Let me just—"

"I know you're booked for the weekend, but I was thinking I could have that attic room. The one Henry had been staying in?"

"I'll have to check with the police first, just to—"

"I mean, it's not like Henry's coming back for the room. And since you can't reach him to find out what the deal is, I'm sure it'll be fine. The police looked it over yesterday, so . . ." He waited expectantly.

The hairs on the back of my neck stood up. Something Steve had said was bothering me. Everyone knew that Henry had gone. But no one knew we'd been unable to reach him. I had to think fast.

"Look, I'll pay for the room. That way you'll even come out ahead."

I nodded. "Sure. I can get you set up in the attic room."

He instantly looked relieved.

"But I'll have to get in there and clean it first."

Steve frowned. "That's not really necessary. The kid was only in there one night."

That made the hairs on the back of my neck stand up even more. Who would want to stay in a room that hadn't even had a change of sheets?

"No, I really insist you let us clean the room first. We'll just put fresh linens on the bed and in the bathroom. It won't take long."

Steve started to say something, but then closed his mouth. "I, uh, okay. That'll be fine."

I nodded. "Matthew isn't here right now, but he'll be back shortly. He usually helps me clean the rooms."

Steve sighed, clearly impatient. "Can I at least go ahead and move my things in there?"

"The room is locked up tight," I said. "I'd prefer you let us clean up a bit first."

He looked flustered. "The sooner the better, okay?"

"Absolutely."

He nodded and walked briskly back up the stairs. He and his wife must have found the idea of one more night together in the same room intolerable.

After he was gone, Carol peeked into the front room. "I couldn't help overhearing," she whispered, coming over to the desk. "Wonder why Steve's moving out of his room?" When I hesitated to answer out of professional courtesy to Steve, Carol leaned a little closer. "The way he and Juliet have been fighting, I'm not surprised. But it's suspicious, the way he's in such a hurry to get into Henry's old room. Don't you think?"

I paused and then admitted that it did seem strange. It seemed to me that if Steve was so anxious to get away from his wife, if their marital problems were that serious, he'd pack up and leave. It seemed odd to go on with a vacation when they were clearly on the outs and their home was only a short distance from Williamsbridge.

I took out my phone to text Matthew and see when he'd be home. "I need to get in there and clean the room before Steve moves in," I told Carol.

"For more reasons than one," she whispered, reading my thoughts.

"Just in case there are any clues to be found in the room," I said, nodding.

"Let me help," she said. "We can clean the room up together and search it top to bottom while we're at it."

"We aren't likely to find anything. Detective Dunlap and Officer Potts went over the room yesterday."

"Those two couldn't find a clue if it came up and bit them on the nose," said Carol. "No offense," she added quickly.

"None taken," I assured her. "They do tend to bumble around a lot."

"Stacey and I saw them check that attic room yesterday. They were in and out in two minutes. They barely glanced at it. They were more focused on your mother's baked goods and coffee." She snorted. "Heck, we would've gone in there and checked the room ourselves, but they locked it behind them."

"Matthew and I have actually helped them solve a few cases before," I told her, taking out my master key.

It was true. Not to brag, but we'd been instrumental in two different murder investigations. Don't get me wrong. Dunlap and Potts were fine on their own when it came to everyday crimes. When someone had stolen three pies right off the counter at Bread and Butter, our local bakery, Dunlap and Potts caught the thief in no time. When Doris Blessing claimed that someone had stolen her dog, Scooter, Dunlap and Potts located the missing dog who, as it turned out, had just gone for a galivant around town. But they found him within an hour. If someone parked in a no-parking zone or failed to pay a fine, Dunlap and Potts were on it. But murder? Well, that was a different story.

The more I was getting to know Carol Blake, the more I liked her. "Okay," I said, stepping out from behind the desk. "Let's go see what we can find."

Chapter Fourteen

Carol ended up being a big help. She'd pulled the linens off the bed and put on fresh ones before I'd even finished vacuuming the small attic room. We went into the tiny bathroom together and checked every drawer and cabinet, cleaning as we went along.

"So, this isn't the first time there's been a murder in connection with your inn, is it?" asked Carol. It was a question, but something in her tone told me that she already knew the answer.

"There was a death at a family reunion here last Christmas. And then in February, there was another one." I swallowed the lump in my throat. "And now this with Leonard. Even if he wasn't found dead here at the inn, I'm so afraid that what happened to him will be lumped in with our mystery weekend and our reputation will be ruined. I know that sounds petty. Or disrespectful. The truth is, I didn't know Leonard very well at all. He was known around town as keeping to himself and being grumpy. I guess he wasn't the kind of person you'd get to know well. Anyway, now I'm worried that no one in their right mind will want to come and stay here."

"Are you kidding? Why do you think Stacey and I even found this little place?" When I looked at her blankly, she added, "We read about you in the news."

"You read that there had been two murders here, and that made you *want* to come for a visit?"

Carol nodded. "In a way. We never would've visited your website in the first place if you hadn't been in the news. Then once we made it to your website, and checked out your social media, we learned about the murder mystery weekend, and we were sold."

"Really?" I was shocked. "I assumed that people would start avoiding us, with all the negative press."

"Not necessarily." Carol closed the last cabinet door and we went back into the bedroom. "I'm not saying it's a good thing that these tragedies have happened here—don't get me wrong. But what I *am* saying is that you should reframe your perception and use the inn's history—even the bad stuff—to your advantage."

"Matthew and I are both writers, but we're not experts at marketing. We're sort of winging it."

"You're doing a good job for the most part. You're clearly a good team. Very creative. Some of your posts are perfectly on point. And your website is very well done. I think the only place where you're lacking is the piece about actually getting folks to the social media pages and the website in the first place. That's where these murders come in. This latest one, well . . . Let me emphasize again that it's awful that this has happened—that anyone has died. But this is national news at this point."

"But how—"

"You're a journalist, aren't you? So, write the story about the little inn with a curse. Link your website. Don't play it as a publicity stunt. Present it as a point of interest." She winked at me. "Trust me. It's news. And in the right light, it won't hurt you a bit. On the contrary."

"Are you—I mean, you seem to know a lot about this kind of thing."

"Why do you think Stacey and I go all over the world to these murder mystery events?"

"I thought it was just a hobby or something. I thought you were filthy rich and just did this for fun."

"We *are* filthy rich. But it's because we're the authors of the blog and internationally syndicated column—"

"*Undercover Sisters*!" I hadn't meant to blurt it out so loudly, but it all made sense now. "I thought you looked familiar! I've read some of your articles. You've written a couple of books, too. I can't believe you're here at our little inn!"

Carol smiled. "We don't generally broadcast our identity, but we don't hide it either. We play along—you know, two well-to-do sisters, world travelers . . . I know we come off a little snooty. We play our parts as a way of keeping our distance. We like to observe and write our columns from the point of view of regular customers. If our hosts knew who we were, they might give us special treatment, and that would affect the integrity of the writing."

"That makes sense."

"We've felt so at home at Pumpkin Hill, though. We truly think this place is a gem. We'll definitely be giving you a glowing review."

"That's amazing. How do I even begin to thank you?"

"No need," Carol said with a laugh. "Just keep doing what you're doing, and—"

Suddenly a phone rang.

"Is that yours?" Carol asked.

"Nope, it must be yours," I said, glancing at my cell phone.

"It's not mine."

We both looked around. The ringing was coming from under the bed. I knelt down, and sure enough, just under the dust ruffle, tucked in behind the bedside table, was a cell phone. I grabbed it and answered it before it stopped ringing.

"Hello?"

There was a pause. "Who's this?"

"My name is Eloise Lewis. I'm the innkeeper at the Inn at Pumpkin Hill."

"What are you doing with Henry's phone?"

"Oh—is this Henry Schmidt's phone? I just found it under his bed."

"Oh. This is Megan. I'm Henry's girlfriend. Can I speak to Henry, please?"

I looked at Carol, who, of course, couldn't hear the conversation so she probably wondered why I looked so worried. "Henry's not here. He checked out unexpectedly. I guess he accidentally left his phone behind."

"Oh no." Megan's breathing got heavier, and she was clearly upset.

"What is it? What's wrong?"

"Henry called me last night. He was afraid he was in some kind of danger. He called while I was at work, and I just now found his message. But he sounded really scared."

"Did he say what he was afraid of?"

"All he said was that there'd been a murder and that

he felt he was in danger. He asked me to call him back and I didn't, and he must've wondered why." She sounded anguished. "I feel so terrible. My stupid ringer was off and I worked late, then went home and fell asleep watching T.V. It occurred to me that it was strange that he hadn't called to check in, but he'd seemed excited about the murder mystery thing when I'd talked to him earlier in the day, and I just thought he must be off having a good time. I should've checked my phone!"

"Maybe he's on the way home right now and just can't call you because he lost his phone," I offered.

She paused. "Maybe. But I have a bad feeling about this."

I took down her number, and we agreed to call each other if either of us heard from Henry. I got off the phone and brought Carol up to speed.

"Well, my bet is on Steve White," she said decisively.

"Steve? What do you mean? Steve knows where Henry is?" I paused. "Or do you think Steve is the murderer . . ."

"I think Steve is part of this whole thing. There was

that whole business with the blood on his shirt. And why is he so anxious to get into this room? He didn't even want you to clean it first. He must be looking for that!" She pointed at Henry's cell phone.

"So, you think he knows Henry forgot his phone? But that would mean . . ."

"That would mean Henry was afraid for good reason, that Steve knows where Henry is, that he knows he doesn't have his phone . . ."

"And that he's worried someone else will find it before he does." I tucked the phone into my pocket.

Carol nodded. "We just need to find a way to prove it."

Chapter Fifteen

As soon as Matthew returned from running errands, he, Carol, Stacey and I sat down for a quiet chat in the kitchen. It was a rare moment when we had the inn all to ourselves. Steve was on the front porch, absorbed in a book. Juliet had gone for a walk in the woods. The Frys had joined the Stokes for lunch at Potbelly's, and the O'Connors were outside, picking their perfect pumpkin on the hillside. The rest of the group had decided to go around the village hunting for more clues. Someone said something about trying to find out who all had it in for Leonard, and I felt pretty sure the various shop and restaurant owners would be happy to humor them since everyone wanted to find out who'd killed Leonard—and everyone knew that our blundering police force needed all the help it could get.

Carol and I filled Matthew and Stacey in on Steve wanting Henry's room so badly and our finding Henry's phone and talking to his girlfriend Megan. We pondered ways of proving that Steve had something to do with Henry going missing. We had differing views about what to do next, but we all agreed on one thing. Steve's behavior was suspect. He shouldn't have known that we couldn't reach Henry. And it was odd that he was in such a rush to move into Henry's old room. And then there was the mysterious bloody nose that day of Leonard's death—*had that only been the day before yesterday?*

"I've got it," said Matthew. "We're making this too complicated."

We all leaned forward to hear Matthew's idea.

"If our hunch is right and Steve knows where Henry is right now, let's just go out there on the front porch and tell Steve he can have Henry's room—that we just got a call from Henry telling us he'd left his phone behind—"

"That's it!" I said. "If Steve wants Henry's phone,

he'll rush up to the room to find it and we'll have confirmation that Steve has something to hide. And if he leaves the inn right away, we'll know that *he* knows that Henry shouldn't be in a position to call anyone, and he'll have to go and check on Henry."

"Exactly." Matthew frowned. "I think."

"Brilliant!" said Carol. "Let's do it."

A few minutes later, I walked out onto the front porch and approached Steve. The Blake sisters sat casually flipping through magazines by the fire, and Matthew took his post at the front desk.

"Good news," I said. Steve looked up from his book. "The attic room is all ready for you. You can go ahead and move in there. I'm, um, sorry if you and your wife are having a rough time."

"Oh. No, we're fine. It's just . . . I've been having my usual fall hay fever, and I snore horribly. I just thought it would be nice for Juliet to be able to get some sleep tonight." He jumped up from his chair and led the way back into the front room.

"Oh good. You're here," said Matthew, hanging up

the phone at the desk. "I just heard from Henry. He told me he thinks he left his cell phone here."

"Really? That's funny. I haven't seen it around." I turned to Steve. "Steve, be sure to keep an eye out for it when you're settled in the attic room. Maybe it's in there somewhere. We gave it such a quick cleaning, we probably overlooked it."

Steve, who had turned very pale, just swallowed and then managed to nod. "I, uh—of course. I'll let you know if I find it." He looked toward the staircase. "You know, I think I'll move my things into the room a little later, though. I just remembered something. I had ordered lunch for Juliet and me down in town, and I was supposed to pick it up. I'd better head down there."

"I can give the restaurant a call if you'd like," I said. "Where did you order from?"

"Oh—no, that's okay." He glanced at his watch. "I'll just run on down there."

He practically ran through the front door. Matthew and I looked into the adjoining family room at the Blake sisters, who were wearing matching excited expressions on their faces.

MURDER MYSTERY AT THE INN

"Well, don't just stand there," Carol said, jumping up from the couch. "He's getting away!"

The moment Steve had driven down the hill, we all jumped into the inn's jeep and followed him, keeping a bit of distance between us and hoping he was too focused on where he was going to look back much. Williamsbridge is a small town. It's not easy to drive around incognito there. Once we'd followed Steve over William's Other Bridge and out Gunther Hill Road, southeast of town, it got even harder to stay hidden. Matthew dodged behind the occasional other car that we came across, and we all kept our eyes peeled to make sure we never completely lost sight of Steve's car.

"Where did you say the Whites are from?" asked Matthew, glancing over at me.

"Settlersville. It's a tiny town toward Waterbury."

"Well, that seems to be where we're headed," said Matthew.

"So, you think Steve's going to his own house?" asked Stacey from the backseat.

"That's my best guess," said Matthew.

Sure enough, within a few more minutes, we'd entered the Settlersville town limit. Steve made a few more turns, going down a country lane and finally pulling up at what appeared to be an old, abandoned barn. He got out of his car and ran inside. Matthew pulled the jeep in behind a large clump of bushes.

"Call Dunlap and Potts," he said. "We really shouldn't storm this place without backup. Who knows what the situation is inside."

"Already done," I said, holding up my phone. "I texted them when we came this way. They're only a few minutes behind us. I've been sending Dunlap a message every time we've made a turn."

Matthew shook his head at me, smiling. "You really are amazing," he said.

Once again, my cheeks felt hot and my heart raced, and it wasn't just because of the excitement of the case.

A few short minutes later, Dunlap and Potts drove right past us, giving us a wave. They parked in front of the barn, and hopped out of their police cruiser.

We heard Dunlap yelling, "Mr. White, we'd like a

word with you. This is Detective Dunlap." He banged on the door.

We all climbed out of our jeep and edged closer to the barn.

"Mr. White, I think you'd better come on out here," Dunlap said sternly. "Otherwise, we'll have to come in."

A few moments passed, and then the barn door slowly slid open and a defeated-looking Steve came out.

Dunlap and Potts pulled him aside, and the rest of us rushed into the barn, where we found poor Henry, tied to a post, looking frightened and confused but otherwise unharmed.

"Thank goodness you're okay," I said, kneeling in the hay beside Henry as Matthew untied him.

"He didn't hurt me," said Henry, nodding, but trembling. "Just scared me."

"You poor thing," said Carol.

"Here, I have a bottle of water," said Stacey, handing Henry her bottle.

He took a long drink. "Steve told me he knew the

police were going to be questioning me a lot. He didn't want them to do that. He was afraid I'd remember—"

"Everything okay in here?" asked Dunlap, coming inside the barn.

"Henry's here. He's fine," I said.

"Good, good," said Dunlap. "I'm glad you're okay, young man. Your father's been worried sick."

"Ready to go, sir?" Potts stuck his head into the open doorway.

Dunlap nodded toward Potts. "Listen," he said, turning back to Henry. "We're going to book White for kidnapping you and probably for the murder of your Uncle Leonard." He pointed at me and Matthew and the Blake sisters. "You lot look after Henry here and bring him over to the station. We need to get a statement from you about what's been going on out here."

Henry nodded, and Dunlap and Potts jumped back into their cruiser and drove away with Steve safely tucked into the backseat.

The rest of us walked slowly back over to the jeep.

"So, why did Steve kidnap you?" I asked, looking at Henry. "You said he was afraid you'd remember something?"

"He knew that when I first arrived in Williamsbridge and went to my uncle's house, I'd seen his wife Juliet there."

"Juliet?" I stopped walking. "What would she be doing at Leonard's house?"

"I didn't know at the time. And to be honest, I wasn't even sure it *was* Juliet White until I'd seen her again several times at the inn. I'm not great at remembering faces. But it was her. She was at Leonard's, and neither of them looked very happy. They'd been arguing."

"What about?" asked Matthew.

"I've had a lot of time to think about all of this while I've been tied up in this barn, and it all makes sense now."

"Go on," said Carol, putting a reassuring hand on Henry's arm.

"I finally remembered something from many years ago. Uncle Leonard was visiting Dad and me. I was just a kid—like around eleven or twelve. I heard the two of them arguing. Dad kept saying the name *Juliet*, and talking about how Leonard had had an affair with her, and that she'd had his child—a son. Dad was furious with Leonard, saying he needed to step up and help Juliet. You know, do the right thing. But Leonard refused."

"So that was the conflict over their moral values that Richard talked about," I said, finally understanding. "And now that you mention it, I remember when Leonard checked you into the inn. He kept looking into the family room, frowning. I'd be willing to bet he'd spotted Juliet—a ghost from his past."

"A skeleton in his closet," added Matthew.

Henry nodded. "And Steve thought I'd recognized Juliet and would tell the cops about her connection to Leonard . . . and I guess that would make the Whites suspects in the murder."

"So, Leonard had an affair with Juliet, and Steve killed him to get revenge?" Matthew wondered.

"But the Whites said their son is twelve years old," I said. "So, the affair happened twelve years ago. Why would Steve wait until now to get his revenge?"

"Maybe he just found out?" said Stacey.

"Maybe they had a fight—maybe that's why Steve had the bloody nose," said Carol.

"Maybe," I said. But something still bothered me. "It seems to me that there are two people who might have reason to want Leonard dead. One of them is Steve . . ."

"And he's in custody," said Matthew, opening the door to the jeep.

"But what if he's not the murderer?"

Chapter Sixteen

We all got into the jeep and rushed back to Williamsbridge, only a few minutes behind Potts and Dunlap. On the drive, I called Mom and told her where we were and what had happened.

"Mom, do me a favor. Tell Juliet that her husband has been taken into custody and see how she reacts, okay?"

Mom agreed and promised to call me back if she had anything to report.

I felt more at ease the moment we crossed over William's Other Bridge and headed toward the town square where the little police station sat next to the courthouse.

"Dunlap and Potts must've hit a few red lights on the way home," said Matthew. "Look, they just pulled into the station."

My phone rang. "It's Mom," I said, taking the call. "Hi, Mom."

"Eloise, you should know that Juliet acted very strangely when I gave her the news about Steve. I mean, you'd expect a wife to be upset by something like that, but this was different. She hightailed it into town just a moment ago. Literally went running down the hill at top speed. I think she's probably headed for the station."

At that very moment, I saw Juliet flying down Court Street. She arrived in the parking lot and bent over, hands on her knees, breathless.

"Wow," I said. "Good thing Pumpkin Hill is so close."

"What? Why?" asked Matthew. Then he saw Juliet. "Oh. Wow."

"Mom, Juliet's here at the station. Gotta go. Thank you!"

"Eloise, don't do anything dangerous—" I hung up before she finished her sentence.

All at once, I could see Detective Dunlap and Officer Potts helping Steve out of the backseat of the cruiser, and Juliet catching her breath and charging toward them.

"Dunlap!" I screamed. "Potts!" My first instinct was that Juliet had a concealed weapon of some kind and was rushing to her husband's rescue, and that the hapless Dunlap and Potts were in grave danger.

The two of them looked at me, and I pointed to Juliet, who was almost upon them by then.

"Stand back, ma'am!" said Potts, reaching toward his gun.

"Not another step!" said Dunlap at the same time.

Juliet stopped short, surprising us all by falling to her knees, sobbing. I walked over to her.

"Juliet?"

"You have the wrong person!" Juliet cried, pointing at her husband.

"What are you talking about, Mrs. White?" asked Dunlap.

Juliet put her face into her hands.

"Steve didn't kill Leonard, did he?" I asked, keeping my voice quiet.

Juliet shook her head but said nothing. By that time, Stacey, Carol, Henry, and Matthew had all gathered round.

"You and my uncle," Henry started to say.

Juliet looked up at him, her eyes glistening with tears. "I'm so sorry."

"Wait just a second here," said Potts.

"Juliet, you don't have to do this," said Steve.

"No, it's time I told the truth," said Juliet, looking sadly at her husband. "It's way past time. And there's no way you're taking the fall for what I did."

"Will someone please tell me what's going on here?" said Dunlap, who was starting to turn red in the face.

Juliet took a deep breath. "A little over twelve years

ago, I had an affair." She swallowed. "With Leonard Schmidt."

Steve took a step forward. "Juliet—"

"I had a close friend who was getting married. We came to Williamsbridge for her bachelorette weekend. I met Leonard at a bar just outside of town. I'd had too much to drink." She sniffled. "You know. Same old story. But one good thing came of that terrible mistake. I had a son about nine months later." Juliet locked eyes with her husband again. "Steve didn't even suspect." She began to cry again. "All this time . . ."

"But why did you decide to reconnect with Leonard this weekend?" I asked.

"For a while now, I've been wanting to get some family background—you know, health information. Our pediatrician is always asking about genetic conditions our son might be predisposed to, and when Steve and I decided to come to Williamsbridge for the murder mystery thing, and we passed Leonard's Repair Shop on our way into town . . . and then I saw him checking Henry into the inn . . . Well, I thought I could approach Leonard and ask him about his family's health background. And then, well, part of me just wanted to see him again. To tell him that I hated him for disregarding his own son. The other part of me wanted to pretend the whole affair had never happened and leave it in the past." She let out a deep breath. "I knew he might not be glad to see me, but I didn't think he'd be mean." She shook her head. "He was awful. Cold as ice. Told me to keep my mouth shut and get out. That he didn't care about the child I'd had as a result of our affair. In that moment, I hated him. And I hated myself. I grabbed a mallet from his workbench and hit him in the head." She looked at Dunlap and Potts. "I swear I didn't mean to kill him. I was just so . . . enraged."

Steve, still in handcuffs, walked toward his wife. The look on his face was heartbreaking. He was clearly torn between his own hurt and his love for his wife, even in the face of her betrayal. "Juliet, we'll get through this. We'll figure this out."

"And Steve here," Juliet went on, motioning toward her husband, "is such a decent person that he tried to cover my tracks. He even changed the clues in those envelopes to spare me having to return to that shop after what I'd done." She stood and stepped closer to

Steve. "I had no idea you'd followed me to Leonard's Repair Shop that afternoon. Steve, I'm so ashamed."

"Steve had a bloody nose that night," I remembered. "What was that about?"

"That was nothing—"

"He fell," Juliet said, interrupting Steve. "He saw what I did and was so shocked, he got dizzy and fell and bloodied his nose. We even argued about it the next day when I saw the blood on his shirt. I was about to confess then, but he wanted to protect me. He helped me clean up the mess, and we left." She looked at Henry again. "We left your uncle lying there, all alone. He was dead, so there was no point calling an ambulance. And then that night, when we were all out hunting for clues, we saw you go into his shop. Steve knew you'd be there, you see, because he'd switched my clue with yours. Anyway, that's when we decided to frame you for Leonard's death."

"It was a horrible thing to do," said Steve, taking a step toward Henry. "We were desperate. And in shock. We didn't think they'd be able to prove you'd done it, and all we could think about was getting home to our son."

Henry stood there, wide-eyed and speechless like the rest of us.

"Let's go inside. Both of you," said Dunlap, taking Steve's arm again.

Potts took Juliet's. "You're going to have to tell us this whole story over again. And Henry, you come along too. We'll call your dad and get him over here."

They all walked quietly into the police station with Dunlap and Potts.

"Wow," said Stacey, watching after them. "This has been the most exciting weekend ever."

"The Case of the Broken Repairman," said Carol, nodding in agreement. "Solved."

Chapter Seventeen

The Blake sisters decided to extend their stay at the inn until Tuesday, so that they could relax and enjoy the village before heading off on their next adventure.

"I've got you all set up with reservations for dinner at the Duck and Pheasant." I walked into the family room, where Carol and Stacey had cozied up on the couch with the mystery novels from their goodie bags. "They're expecting you at seven. And we'll be showing spooky Halloween movies back here later tonight, with s'mores by the fireplace."

"Perfect!" said Carol. She and Stacey exchanged a glance. "Eloise, could you come sit a minute?"

"Of course," I said, taking a seat in the fluffy reading chair.

Stacey presented me with a thin stack of pages. "Hot off the presses!" she sang. "We wanted you to have a copy in print."

I looked at the top page and read the title aloud. "*Follow the Clues Straight to Williamsbridge, Vermont.*" I felt a lump form in my throat as I skimmed the glowing review the sisters had posted on their travel blog. They called the Inn at Pumpkin Hill a five-star must-stay, and spoke about how well organized and fun the murder mystery event had been, even in the face of actual tragedy. They said they'd had the adventure of a lifetime and that they would be returning to the inn year after year to participate in our mystery weekends. I was overcome with gratitude. "This is amazing. I don't know how to thank you."

"No need," said Carol with a smile. "We just report what we see."

"And since we posted that story less than an hour ago, it's already received about three thousand hits."

"Three thousand—are you kidding me? We're lucky

if a few *hundred* people see our social media posts in a *month*!"

"You're going to have plenty of business pretty soon," said Stacey, giggling. "And you won't have to worry too much about no one seeing your posts anymore. You're going to be booked solid!"

"And it's all because two wayfaring sisters happened to see an article about two murders connecting you to the inn," said Carol. "See, you just have to reframe things, give them a positive spin. There's almost always a bright side. And while there's nothing good about actual murder, there is something to be said for name recognition."

"I can safely say that I speak for my mother and Matthew when I tell you that this means so much to us." I held up the pages of the blog.

"Well, keep in mind that if we'd shown up here and your service and facilities hadn't been exceptional, we wouldn't have given you our stamp of approval. You earned every word." Carol stood and looked at her sister. "Let's get over to the Duck and Pheasant. I saw a paella on their menu the other night and have been craving it ever since. And there was lobster risotto and an apple galette for dessert that looked wonderful."

"And that poached pear, goat cheese, and pomegranate salad!" said Stacey, standing and slinging her bag over her shoulder. "Let's go!"

The two sisters left the inn and walked down the hill, chattering on about who would order what so they could share and taste everything.

I smiled, watching them go, clutching the pages in my hands and feeling a sudden sense of relief wash over me. The inn was going to be okay. The phone rang at the front desk, and I grabbed it—then felt joy bubbling up as I booked the first customer who'd read all about the inn on the *Undercover Sisters* blog.

After getting off the phone, I hurried into the kitchen, checked the timer on the oven, and breathed in the comforting scent of the pot roast that had been cooking for hours. I slid the large pan out of the oven and popped in the loaf of bread that had been on its final rise for the past hour. Thirty minutes later, Mom, Doc, Matthew, and I sat down to a table loaded with comfort food.

"Eloise, this is wonderful," said Mom, beaming from her seat next to Doc.

"Well, I wanted to make up for last time," I said, plating the meat and roasted vegetables before taking my seat.

"Who knew you could cook?" Matthew teased, earning him a swat with my napkin.

We passed around bread and salad and wine. We toasted the Blake sisters' blog, and the inn, and the future. We let the answering machine pick up incoming calls for the whole meal, and just enjoyed each other's company, knowing that with every ring of the phone, the inn's success was further solidified.

"Just think of all the free time we'll have now that we don't have to spend hours trying to come up with ways to get people to come to the inn," said Matthew, leaning over toward me.

"I can finally get back to doing what I love most," I said, thinking of all the ways I could take the Miss Smithers column to the next level, inspired by the Blakes' writing success.

Matthew raised a brow. "And what would that be?"

I felt my cheeks turning pink. "Oh, you know. Just . . . my writing."

Matthew caught my eyes and held them a moment. "What's your secret, El?" he finally said in a low voice.

"My—what are you talking about?"

He answered that question with a smile. "Are you going to make me get out the Wonder Woman lasso of truth, then? Is that the only way to get you to fess up?"

Doc suddenly stood, saving me from answering. "I'm actually really glad we're all here together," he said, then cleared his throat.

"Ian? What is it?" Mom asked, setting down her fork.

"I was going to wait to do this until the end of the meal—and it is a wonderful meal, Eloise." He gave me a quick, nervous smile. "But the truth is, I've waited long enough."

"Ian—" Mom started to say.

"I wouldn't have you think I'm an impatient man, June," he gently said to my mother. "But there's only so much waiting a man can . . ." He looked at her, his eyes full of tenderness. "The thing is, I think I've loved you since we were kids."

Tears sprung to Mom's eyes and a huge smile spread over her face.

"And you loved my best friend. And you married him. And I was glad. I loved you both. And I promise you, I would never try to take the place of Ben. But June, sometimes love comes around a second time. And the thing is, I want to marry you."

Tears now rolled down Mom's smiling cheeks and she laughed. "Oh, Ian. I want to marry you, too."

"You do?" Doc sat back down and took Mom's hands in his. "You do!"

Mom sighed, beaming. "I do."

There was a moment of complete and utter silence then, which I normally would've noticed. But instead, I was wholly engulfed in the joy in that room. I felt the warmth of Matthew's hand, slipping over mine. I felt the peace of knowing that sometimes everything really did work out, just as it should—that maybe the things that mattered the most in life weren't as fragile as I'd once feared, but were instead resilient. Invincible. Like love itself.

There would be time for planning the perfect wedding, for thinking about the business of the inn and my newspaper column. There would be time to mourn what had been lost and face new challenges. And time to wonder why I didn't want Matthew to move his hand away from mine.

But all of those thoughts could come later. For the rest of that evening, I felt the circle of my family close around me, and resolved to hold on fast to the gifts of the day, realizing, finally, that they were more than enough.

June and Eloise's Pumpkin Pie Spice Balls

Ingredients

1 pumpkin pie, homemade or store-bought (You can also use leftover pie.)

1 package of chocolate or vanilla melting wafers/almond bark (Or choose both flavors if you'd like!)

Favorite fall spices, like cinnamon and nutmeg (optional)

Sprinkles

Dump the whole pie into a bowl and stir it around until it's all mixed together. Sprinkle in a few more spices to taste, if you'd like. Stir it all together and

JUNE AND ELOISE'S PUMPKIN PIE SPICE BALLS

chill in the refrigerator for about half an hour. Form the "dough" into balls and return them to the refrigerator while you melt the almond bark/melting wafers according to the directions on the package. If you're using vanilla almond bark, you can get fancy and add food coloring to make different fall colors. Line a cookie sheet with waxed paper. Dip each pumpkin pie ball to coat and set on the waxed paper. (Eloise usually uses a fork for dipping, and lets the excess coating drip back into the bowl.) Add the sprinkles before the coating hardens. Enjoy!

Author's Note

I'd love to hear your thoughts on my books, the storylines, and anything else that you'd like to comment on —reader feedback is very important to me. My contact information, along with some other helpful links, is listed on the next page. If you'd like to be on my list of "folks to contact" with updates, release and sales notifications, etc.… just shoot me an email and let me know. Thanks for reading!

Also…

… if you're looking for more great reads, Summer Prescott Books publishes several popular series by outstanding Cozy Mystery authors.

Contact Summer Prescott Books Publishing

Twitter: @summerprescott1

Bookbub: https://www.bookbub.com/authors/summer-prescott

Blog and Book Catalog: http://summerprescottbooks.com

Email: summer.prescott.cozies@gmail.com

YouTube: https://www.youtube.com/channel/UCngKNUkDdWuQ5k7-Vkfrp6A

And…be sure to check out the Summer Prescott Cozy Mysteries fan page and Summer Prescott Books Publishing Page on Facebook – let's be friends!

CONTACT SUMMER PRESCOTT BOOKS PUBLISHING

To download a free book, and sign up for our fun and exciting newsletter, which will give you opportunities to win prizes and swag, enter contests, and be the first to know about New Releases, click here: http://summerprescottbooks.com

Printed in Great Britain
by Amazon